EDMUND+OCTAVIA

THE
DULCIE CHAMBERS
MYSTERIES

BY KERRY J CHARLES

BOLT FROM THE BLUE

A Dulcie Chambers Mystery

Kerry J Charles

EDMUND+OCTAVIA

Cover Image: *Sewing Woman* 1890, Harriet Backer.
This image is in the public domain.

ISBN-13: 978-0-9997410-1-6

Edmund+Octavia Publishing, Falmouth, Maine, USA

For Shirley
Thank you… for everything!

CONTENTS

There are connoisseurs of blue
just as there are connoisseurs of wine.

~ Sidonie-Gabrielle Colette

CHAPTER ONE

Cerulean. It was an odd name for an odd color. No one seemed to know the exact shade that the word cerulean represented. The name came from Latin *caelulum*, which came from *caelum*, meaning heaven or sky. In a box of crayons it was a bright, medium-blue, and yet the worldwide, self-proclaimed arbiter of color, Pantone, considered it to be a much lighter shade. The beautiful little Cerulean Warbler combined all the shades, so was equally as nondefinitive.

The pigment named cerulean wasn't actually discovered until two centuries after the word first appeared in the English vocabulary, and that was probably well after it had evolved from an elysian reference to a description of a color.

The ambiguity probably had something to do with why Bella liked the color so much. Undoubtedly, it was her favorite. It represented the sky, and the sky was constantly changing, wasn't it?

It was not unlike her life, a constant change from one foster home to the next, one school to the next, until she finally reached the official age of adulthood, or at least what society defined as the age of adulthood. The chronology wasn't important. Bella had long considered herself to be an adult already. In fact, she wasn't even sure if she had actually had a childhood.

Some people would find that sad, but it never seemed to bother her very much. It was just her life. Everyone is brought up differently, and being an orphan was just her own experience. She hadn't been unhappy, certainly – enough people had been kind and helpful to her – but was the opposite true? Had she really ever been happy?

Following her high school graduation, which she had not attended because there didn't seem to be much point, Bella had been able to go to design school in New York City on a full scholarship. Once there, she had known immediately that she had found her place in the world. She loved the fabrics, to the point where she almost considered them to be her friends. The velvets, velours and corduroys were the soft, comforting ones. The denims and sturdy cottons were the practical, hard-workers. The brocades and silks were the prima donnas and the show-offs. They each had their own personality, and their colors, prints, or patterns just added more dimension. It was her favorite part about designing clothes.

Her least favorite part was the fact that, although fashion design was inherently a creative endeavor, it was also highly competitive. Not to mention subjective, as well. And firmly grounded on the concept of turning a profit. For Bella, it was too much and she began to question whether she could actually make a career for herself in a world that she both loved and despised.

Everything changed on one fateful night. She had been working late on an assignment in one of the school classrooms. She remembered her stomach growling, insisting that it was, indeed, suppertime. A commotion in the hallway distracted her from the difficult seam that she was trying to finish so she put down the garment, went over to the door, and quietly opened it.

A man and a woman were hurrying down the corridor but stopped when they saw her. "Can you sew?" the man blurted out.

Bella laughed. "That's why I'm here," she said. She saw the woman exhale heavily.

"Are you free this evening? I mean, right now?" the man continued. He spoke with a strong British accent.

Bella looked around behind her at her work. Now was as good a time as any to stop for the evening. It would all be there again tomorrow. She turned back to the agitated couple staring at her and nodded, but then realized that she had no idea who they were or what they wanted.

As if reading her mind, the woman said. "We are with the British Royal Opera Company of Covent

Garden, which has its opening performance tonight," she looked at her watch pointedly, "In just over two hours, to be exact. Our lead tenor in the performance has fallen ill suddenly and his costumes do not fit the understudy properly. Apparently he decided to take up weightlifting in an effort to 'become more buff' as he put it," the woman added. "He can barely get his arms into the sleeves."

"Not relevant, Francine," the man interjected.

Bella's brow wrinkled. "Don't you have costume staff with your company?" she asked.

"That's the problem," the man replied. "Half of them have come down with some sort of stomach ailment. We don't really know what it is, nor do we have time to look into it."

"Nor do we care at this moment," Francine said. She reached into her purse and pulled out a business card. Handing it to Bella she said, "Here's my card so you'll know we're not two psychos who wandered in off the street. We really do need help, and will certainly pay you for your time."

That was all Bella needed to hear. "Well then, I'm game," she said. "I need to put away my things here first, but I'll be quick. Where is the performance? Can I meet you there?" She didn't feel comfortable simply getting into a cab with two strangers.

"Of course," Francine said quickly. "It's at the Met. Go to the stage door around back and show them my card. They'll be expecting you." The two were already turning to leave.

"Wait!" Bella exclaimed. You don't even know my name!"

They turned back looking sheepish. "Terribly sorry," the man said. "We've been so distraught. Please tell us."

"It's Bella. Bella Washington."

And that had been how it all began.

ભ

"My goodness, Dulcie! Look at you!" The British accent and the smooth, friendly voice was unmistakable to the Maine Museum of Art director, Dr. Dulcinea Chambers. She spun around in her chair and grinned, then jumped up and ran over to the woman, giving her a quick hug.

"Francine Belmont! I can't believe it's you!" Dulcie exclaimed. "How long has it been?" she added.

"Far too long," the woman replied. She adjusted the glasses perched on her head and Dulcie noticed a streak of gray hair that had certainly not been there the last time she had seen her former Oxford professor.

"Then we have lots of catching up to do!" Dulcie said. "How about a coffee? Or would you prefer tea?"

Francine smiled at her friend. "Coffee is fine – I am in America now after all!"

Dulcie's assistant Rachel had been hovering just outside the doorway. "I'm on it!" Dulcie heard her call out. Dulcie looked back at Francine and grinned.

"Quite the efficient staff you have here," Francine commented, then sat in the leather chair that Dulcie gestured toward by her desk.

Walking around the desk and settling in to her own chair, Dulcie put her elbows on the blotter and folded her hands beneath her chin. "And from what I hear, you certainly have an excellent staff as well. What would we do without them?" she said.

"A whole lot more work, I imagine!" Francine replied. Rachel came back in with two steaming mugs of coffee. She slid one in front of Dulcie and put the other carefully down beside her guest. Francine looked into it, then up at Rachel. "How did you know I take cream?" she asked with surprise.

Dulcie smirked. "That is one of Rachel's many mysteries that will never be revealed. She always knows how people take their coffee. I have no idea how she does it."

Rachel tossed her unruly ginger curls over her shoulder. "It's a gift," she said with a mock sigh and left the office, closing the door behind her.

Francine burst out laughing. "Oh, Dulcie! You have no idea how pleased I am that our directors chose your museum as the first stop for our travelling exhibit! *The Costumes of Covent Garden*. It's going to be such fun!"

Dulcie sipped her coffee. "I think you might have had something to do with the choice of location?" she said slyly.

"Well, it was the most logical, certainly. You're in the northeast corner of the US, so the least amount of travel time for all of us getting across the pond. Plus, this is a smaller museum, so we can get the kinks out of the setup process without the fanfare of a big metropolis staring at us. And I must say, your idea of kicking things off with three local performers singing arias in full costume from our exhibit displays was simply genius!" Francine said.

"That's half the fun of doing what I do," Dulcie replied. "Hanging paintings on the walls is only a small part of it. Art can be so many things, and this is yet another example. Besides, who doesn't like a good opera, right?"

Francine rolled her eyes, "Oh, lots of people evidently, given that the board keeps reminding me that our coffers are less than overflowing. They're hoping that this drums up publicity for upcoming shows as much as anything else."

"Then we'll just have to show them all what they're missing," Dulcie said. "Now let's get down to some details," she added, opening her laptop. "And afterward, I'd love to take you to dinner so we can properly chat!"

"I would like nothing better," Francine said.

ᚷ

Dan Chambers wandered around the deck of his small yacht tidying up. He had just returned from yet another cruise around Casco Bay with a group of happy tourists. They'd been in luck today and spotted a whale off in the distance. It had obligingly put on quite a show, slapping its fins and tail flukes against the surface of the chilly Atlantic. That made Dan happy for two reasons: first, he could tell his passengers the latest news on the environmental concerns with the whales, and second, he could start spinning yarns about the old days when the sea captains harpooned the massive creatures. The latter were almost completely made up as he went along, something that the passengers never seemed to mind as long as they were entertained and kept in good supply of cold beverages. As an extrovert, Dan couldn't be happier with his choice of careers.

"Ahoy!" A voice shouted down to him.

Dan looked up to see Detective Nicholas Black standing on the dock, shielding his eyes from the sun and looking back down at him. The tide was out so the yacht sat very low against the pilings.

"Ahoy, yourself!" Dan replied with a halfhearted salute. "C'mon down if you dare!" he added.

Nick clambered down the steep gangplank and joined Dan on the deck. Nick squinted in the late afternoon sun reflecting off the water then remembered that his sunglasses were in his shirt pocket. He pulled them out and slid them on. Much better.

"You look even more like a detective with those things on," Dan said as he continued his work coiling lines on the deck. "Can't imagine you as a lawyer," he commented.

"I never actually was one," Nick said. "I've got the degree but never took the bar. Never wanted to," he said. "And I'm not at all unhappy with the way things have turned out so far," he added.

Dan stopped what he was doing and looked at his friend with mock sincerity. "Just so long as you continue to do right by my sister you'll remain 'not unhappy'," he said. "Cross her, and you'll have me to face!"

Nick laughed. He and Dulcie had become an item, and Nick had no intention of letting anything affect that status. He quite honestly adored her, as her brother Dan was well aware.

"Speaking of," Nick said, "I just got a text from her saying she's having dinner with a colleague tonight. A former professor here from England who's with that new travelling exhibit. So I'm on my own, it seems. Want to go get a beverage and some fried clams?"

"Mmmm! Love to!" Dan said. "Give me about ten more minutes though."

Nick walked over to the cooler on the deck, opened it and plunged his hand into what remained of the ice. He pulled out a can of beer and tossed it to Dan. "Might as well get started, eh?" Nick said.

"I can surely do that," Dan replied. "One of the benefits of my job, or this part anyway: I can drink while I work!"

Nick chuckled as he pulled out a can for himself, cracked it open, and let the cooler lid fall back into place. He then found a comfortable seat on the deck and sat with the sun shining behind him, warming his back. "Ah!" he exhaled, gazing across the water. "And this is why I moved to Maine."

Dan looked over at him. "That it is," he agreed. "Makes you forget all about the brutal winters, doesn't it?"

Nick nodded in response as he took a long swig from the can.

"Hey, is Dulcie's thing that opera exhibit she's been rambling on about?" Dan asked.

"Yep," Nick said. "Actually, it sounds interesting. They're going to do a performance at the opening. Should be good!"

Dan made a grimacing face. "Dulcie's the cultural one. She loves that stuff. I'll go, but not sure I can appreciate the entertainment to the same degree she will."

"As long as you're there, I'm sure that's all she cares about," Nick replied. "You're her alter-ego. Frightens me sometimes," he said.

Nick had made the comment sound humorous, but he was only half-joking. He was looking forward to the day when Dan found a partner in life. Not that Dan was at all a problem or a proverbial fifth-wheel or anything else of the sort. But he was certainly a presence of which Nick was keenly aware, and given the bumpy start to his relationship with Dulcie, Nick wanted to remain on good terms with him. Besides, he actually did consider Dan to be a good friend at this point, independent of Nick's own relationship with Dulcie.

Dan disappeared into the yacht's cabin, then reappeared several moments later with his jacket in hand. He locked the door behind him and tossed his now empty can into the returnables bin on the deck. Nick did the same and followed him up the gangplank.

"Where to?" Dan asked. "The usual?"

Nick grunted his approval. The 'usual' was a waterfront restaurant popular with the locals called Gilbert's. It had just the right balance of fried foods served on waxed paper in plastic baskets, and cold beer in hefty pint glasses.

A seagull hopped along the dock in front of them searching for a stray snack. Another gull flapped down and landed next to it, nosing its beak gently into the first gulls neck. The first one returned the gesture, momentarily forgetting its search for a quick morsel. "Must be his girlfriend," Dan said.

"Wouldn't be surprised," Nick answered. He decided it was a good opening for broaching the subject of Dan's love life. "So when are you going to settle in?" he asked.

"You know, that's a good question," Dan replied. Lately he'd been feeling a bit empty. Maybe it had something to do with turning thirty? Dan had never managed to stay attached to any one girlfriend for very long. Not that he had tried very hard – he hadn't been unhappy to 'play the field' as the saying went. Still, seeing Dulcie and Nick, he had started to realize that maybe his life would be better with someone in it. "Yes," Dan repeated quietly. "That's a very good question."

I am independent!
I can live alone
and I love to work.

~ Mary Cassatt

CHAPTER TWO

It felt strange to be back in America. Bella had lived in London for the past two years, never once returning to the US. She didn't have any need to. She had no family connections and only a few vague friendships, if they could be called that. She had settled in to her new British life well, spending the majority of her time working. That made her happy.

She had never been to Maine but so far she liked it. Portland was a very picturesque place and the people seemed a bit more reserved than in New York. That suited Bella well. She'd never been one to easily mingle with others.

Standing in a basement room of the Maine Museum of Art, she watched as two workers wheeled in several trunks that had just arrived. They were filled with costumes, fabric, and sewing notions – everything that she would need to ensure that the costumes on display were kept in good condition. One trunk even contained her personal sewing machine although she wasn't sure which trunk it was. She'd need to open them all anyway, so it didn't matter – she'd find it soon enough.

When the last trunk was thumped down on the floor, Bella got to work. She shoved them into a neat row, then unlocked them one by one, raising each lid and making note of their contents. A large worktable had been set up at the center of the room, and Bella began to fill it with the notions and tools of her trade. When she located her sewing machine, that joined the rest of the items on the table.

Rachel stuck her head in the door. "Need anything?" she asked.

Bella looked up, startled. She'd been lost in her own little world. "I'd love a cup of tea," Bella said. "Is there a lunchroom or something like that here?" she asked.

Rachel joined her by the table. "You're American, obviously." Rachel could tell from Bella's accent of course. "Did you get acclimated to the tea thing right away?" she asked.

Bella shook her head. "Actually, no. I've been drinking tea for as long as I can remember. I bring it with me everywhere," she added. As if to prove her point, she reached over for her tote bag and pulled out a small tin. She opened it and showed the contents to Rachel. The fragrance of orange pekoe wafted up from a half dozen teabags. Rachel smiled.

"Mmmmm," she said. "I'm definitely a coffee drinker but I have to admit that I do love a cup of tea on occasion. It seems so relaxing."

Bella smiled. It certainly was.

"How about if I go scare up a kettle and a mug or two? You've got a sink in here for water, so you could make tea any time." Rachel said.

"That would be lovely!" Bella replied as Rachel scurried out the door.

Bella didn't really want to go into a lunchroom and try to make conversation with anyone. And as a new person, people would undoubtedly start talking to her, introducing themselves, being friendly. It was of course the socially accepted way of things. Bella had learned to play the game but never felt comfortable doing it. As long as she could stay in her own world, she was content.

"Here you go!" Rachel announced as she returned. She had an electric kettle in one hand, the cord trailing along and bouncing on the floor, and two mugs, each with a spoon, in the other hand. Under her arm were two small plates to put under the mugs and corral the used teabags. Rachel always thought of everything.

"I brought two in case you have company, or, if you're anything like me, you don't feel like washing out one mug over and over. Now you can go through two cups before you have to bother with any washing," she laughed.

"Brilliant!" Bella said. It was exactly the sort of thing she would have done. "But you'll join me for a cup right now, yes?" she asked. She really wanted to get on with her work but felt as though she should be polite.

"I'd love to!" Rachel replied. "But I should earn my keep. Can I help you unpack?"

Bella realized that she and Rachel were similar in that they were dedicated to their jobs. They liked their work and liked to be busy. Bella nodded in agreement. "Why don't you make the tea and I'll organize these things, then I can show you what to do," she offered.

"Perfect plan," said Rachel. A few moments later she handed a steaming mug to the other woman, then took a tentative sip of her own. She looked down at the table. "Oooohhh!" she exclaimed. "That's beautiful!" She ran her hand over a bolt of fabric beside her.

Bella glanced over and saw what had caught Rachel's eye. She wasn't surprised. "That's a cerulean velvet. The tenor who will be performing at the exhibit opening will wear a jacket that I'll be making for him from it. It's my favorite, to be honest. I've always loved cerulean."

"I can see why," Rachel said. "It looks so rich! The color seems to change as the fabric moves in the light, too." She looked from the fabric back up to her new friend. "The opening is only a few days from now, though. You can make an entire costume in that time?"

"Oh absolutely. I've made a jacket in two hours before. I've always been a fast sewer, but you have to be doubly quick when you're working with performers. Alterations need to be done at the last minute if someone changes roles, plus more than a few of them are total divas who don't want to do all the fittings and such. I've learned a lot of shortcuts," she smiled.

They heard footsteps in the hallway and both looked up toward the door. "Ah, I see you've met Rachel!" Francine Belmont came into the room followed by Dulcie. "Bella, let me introduce you to the museum director and a dear friend, Dr. Dulcie Chambers. This is my top seamstress and my assistant, Bella Washington," Francine said.

Dulcie held our her hand and shook Bella's warmly. She stared at her for a moment. Bella had an unusual, ethereal quality about her that Dulcie couldn't quite define. The phrase 'other-worldly' popped into her head. Yes, that was it. There was something almost mystical about her. Perhaps that was why she had been drawn to theater, Dulcie thought. Realizing that she was still staring, and not wanting to be rude, Dulcie hurriedly said, "We're so glad you could come and work with us. I'm looking forward to seeing everything!"

"Bella was just telling me about this fabric," Rachel interjected, running her hand over the blue velvet again. "The color is called ceruuuuulean!" She added, drawing out the word. "Doesn't that sound divine?"

Dulcie laughed. "Absolutely! Beyond divine!" She turned to Francine. "We can have Rachel schedule the performers to come in for fittings. How soon should we do that?" she asked.

Francine looked at Bella. "How soon should we do that?" she repeated.

"Do we have their measurements?" Bella asked.

"Yes, I'll get them to you. They're on my desk," Rachel answered.

"I'll start on the tenor's coat first," Bella replied, thinking out loud.

"That's the ceruuuulean!" Rachel said in a loud stage whisper.

Bella laughed and continued, "So if he could come in day after tomorrow, that would be perfect. Then the soprano on the next day, and the baritone the day after that. I should be able to get everything finished up in plenty of time that way."

"Great, I'll get on that!" Rachel said. "It works out well too because from what I hear, the tenor and the soprano can't stand each other so if everyone's on a different day, that makes life easier."

"Oh my, yes. Life in the theater!" Francine said, rolling her eyes. "Let me guess: they were a couple but had an acrimonious breakup."

"That's it!" Rachel exclaimed.

"Yes, it was kind of the talk of the town for a while during the winter," Dulcie added. "Things get kind of slow and dull around here in January and February. The gossips are on overdrive then."

"Every city becomes a small town in the dead of winter," Francine said. "It happens in London, too."

"We'll keep them separated as much as possible then." Dulcie concluded. "All right, if you're all set with everything here Bella, we'll leave you to it."

Bella nodded and the others filed out. "I'll get those measurements to you!" Rachel called out from the hallway.

"Thank you!" Bella called back. She smiled now in the empty room. Empty of people, anyway. All of her 'friends', the yards and yards of fabric, were around her now.

 CR

"Jessica, darling, you are spending far too much time on that dress!"

Devin had decided to visit his wife's studio unannounced. He knew that she loathed when he did that. She now kept her lips pressed tightly together and refused to meet his gaze. It didn't matter as he wasn't looking at her, he was looking at the dress.

An unusual design, it swept from one shoulder down across the dress form in a cascading arc of soft navy silk. An elegant ruffle emerged from the top edge along the shoulder, neck and bust, then diagonally as it accentuated the waist. It continued around and around the wide skirt making it look as though it was moving even when it wasn't.

"You know full well that this dress closes the show, Devin. It has to be perfect. Now what do you want?" The annoyance dripped from her voice as she continued to hand-stitch the ruffle in place.

"I was going to ask you where you wanted to go for dinner, but if you're taking that tone...," he knew she could complete his sentence.

"There isn't time to go out Devin. Just bring me something later. The usual salad will be fine." She still hadn't looked up, but he knew that he'd been dismissed. He silently left.

Jessica waited for a full minute before she glanced at the doorway to make sure that he was actually gone. They'd been at each other's throats for weeks now, every since she had switched to the new designs for her debut collection. It had cost a great deal to buy new fabrics and with Devin financing the launch of her new line as a solo designer, he felt as though he had a say. He had vowed to stay out of the creative aspects of her work, but it was, after all, a business, as he so pointedly continued to remind her. Daily.

Jessica broke off the thread, stuck the needle into the pincushion strapped to her wrist, and stepped back to look at her creation. She was so happy with it. It was beyond beautiful.

A pang of fear wrenched through her body, searing her joy. What if this was her one and only success? What if she could never do this again? She shook her head vigorously as if to clear out the thought. No, she had worked too hard, for too long. Not only would this be a success, there would be many more to come.

Confidence and composure. Those were her words to live by, her daily mantra. She was filled with confidence and composure. If she said it often enough, she might even begin to believe it.

There are no rules.
That is how art is born,
how breakthroughs happen.
Go against the rules or ignore the rules.
That is what invention is about.

~ Helen Frankenthaler

CHAPTER THREE

"The mannequins are arriving late," Rachel announced as she stomped into Dulcie's office.

Dulcie's eyes shot up over the top of her laptop without her head moving. "How late?" she asked.

"Considering they're in Des Moines right now, I can't say," Rachel replied, throwing herself into the chair by Dulcie's desk. "Argh!" she added, either for emphasis or to release her own frustration. Or both.

"Argh, indeed," Dulcie agreed, her eyes sliding back down to the glowing screen in front of her. She tapped the keyboard a few more times, then closed the laptop.

Francine had decided to special-order mannequins from a company in the US and have them shipped to

Portland for the exhibit. From there they would be transported to each new location. It seemed like a good plan, and much less expensive than sending mannequins across the Atlantic from England.

"The best laid plans…," Dulcie said.

Rachel nodded. Her mind was already racing ahead to determine a Plan B. "All right," she said. "What if I check with some more local warehouses to see if there are any that we could rent on short notice, just in case."

"Excellent plan," Dulcie said.

"Who covers the cost?" Rachel asked. She was increasingly involved in the budgets of exhibits since Dulcie realized her assistant had a knack for numbers. She also had the ability to ferret out a good bargain if one was to be had, always a helpful skill.

"Us, I imagine," Dulcie replied. "Francine said they'd buy the mannequins, but since we actually carried out the logistics, I think we own the problem now." She sat back in her chair. "OK, good solution to locate some rentals. Start scoping them out and we'll see what we can do."

"Hey, maybe we could give a rental company some ad space or sponsorship credit or something, and they'd give us a discount!" Rachel was already working her magic.

"Now you're thinking," Dulcie said. "All right, scoot! I have to finish these emails," she added, opening her laptop again.

Rachel was already out the door, eager to jump on this new task. Dulcie heard her giggle out in the hallway, then she heard her brother's voice. She closed her laptop again. "Clearly I'm not going to get anything done this morning," she muttered to herself.

Dan came in and sat in the chair that Rachel had just vacated. "She looked like she was on a mission," he said.

"That she is," Dulcie replied. "We've had our first major problem with the costume exhibit. She's on it, though."

"As always," Dan said. "Navigator," he pointed to Dulcie, "…and tactician." He now pointed out into the hallway.

Dulcie's brow furrowed. "What exactly does that mean?" she asked.

"Navigator and tactician," he repeated. "You need both to move a ship forward efficiently, or a project in this case. The navigator charts the course in advance, but inevitably you'll get blown off in some way, so the tactician figures out how to get you back on track every time as quickly as possible."

Dulcie pursed her lips, thinking. "Huh, that's a great analogy," she finally said.

"Yup, leave it to an old salt like myself," Dan quipped.

Dulcie laughed, as Dan knew she would. She glanced out the window. "So what brings you indoors on a beautiful sunny day? I'd have thought you'd be bringing tourists around the bay."

"Just got back in from the early morning run," Dan said. "Going back out after lunch. And if I can squeeze in a sunset cruise, I'll do that also."

"Busy day!" Dulcie interjected.

"Make hay while the sun shines. And since it's shining for longer hours now that we're finally getting into June, it's potentially a lotta hay!" Dan added. "But that's actually why I'm here. I know you've got a friend and her crew in town right now. Want to take them out on the boat? We could schedule something before it gets too busy for everyone."

"Fabulous idea!" Dulcie exclaimed. "Francine would love it, and I'm sure the seamstress that she brought along would too. There are a few others in their group as well, and then there's Rachel of course."

"And your perpetual date, Nick," Dan added.

Dulcie looked at him pointedly. "Well, duh!" she said. She glanced at her calendar. "Maybe a sunset cruise tomorrow? The head seamstress will have done her first fitting that day, so she could probably use a break after. Will the weather still be good?"

Dan nodded. "Yep, weather's supposed to hold like this for the rest of the week." He stood up. "All right, tomorrow evening it is. How about you round up everyone and get them down to the dock around half past six? I'll have some beverages and snacks ready."

"You are my hero," Dulcie replied.

"I thought Nick was your hero," Dan laughed.

"Yes, he is too. I have a plethora of heroes. I'm just that lucky," she said. She made a shooing motion with her hands. "Thank you so much, but now go. We both have work to do!"

"Fine. Guess the 'hero' status only lasts for so long," he said, sauntering from the room.

Dulcie smirked, shaking her head and focused on her computer again.

ᔕ

Jessica gazed out from her studio window across the busy New York street. She'd eventually gone home the night before but was up again early this morning. She was exhausted but nothing could be done about it. She had to finish. And it had to be perfect.

She felt badly about how she'd spoken to her husband. He had every right to be concerned about the finances. The margins were much tighter now, but it was a calculated risk on her part. The changes were crucial, especially the gown for the finale. Lavish parties were back in vogue. Jessica could picture the gown as a couture item, but also in a simpler, mass-produced version in different colors. Potentially, it could be a money-maker for them.

She rolled the dress form over closer to the window to check her stitchwork from the night before. Everything looked even and, more importantly, hidden. Good. She made a few notes in the sketchbook on how to machine-sew the ruffle trim onto the skirt prior to actually putting together the dress pieces. That would speed production up enormously. Devin would be happy with that.

Her cellphone buzzed with a text message, and she glanced over at it. Devin. He was asking if she wanted something for lunch. She'd been up so early that he'd still been asleep when she left the apartment. She quickly texted back that she'd love a ham and cheese sandwich, then added a smiling emoji with heart eyes. That would make him happy. He replied with an emoji blowing her a kiss. There. They were back on track after the tiny tiff from the night before. Jessica sighed, relieved.

An hour later Devin came in with a bag from the corner deli. "Delivery for a Mrs. Jessica James!" he announced.

She smiled and gave him a quick kiss. "Thank you, I'm famished!" she said.

The papers rustled as they unwrapped their sandwiches and Jessica took a large bite, washing it down with the lukewarm coffee she'd been drinking. Devin picked up her cup as soon as she put it down. "Looks like you need a refresh," he said and disappeared for a few moments.

When he returned he carefully put the cup down, then looked at her pointedly. "I have an idea, and I won't take 'No' for an answer," he said.

His wife stopped chewing and stared at him. It wasn't like Devin to issue ultimatums.

"You need to get away from this, if only for a day," he began.

"Devin, I can't…," she started to say, but he put up his hand, stopping her.

"We're taking a quick, overnight trip up to Portland. I have to meet with someone up there, and I just saw that there's a costume exhibit about to open at the Maine Museum of Art. The person I'm meeting with is on the board, so I think I can get you a sneak peek preview of the exhibit. The whole thing would take 24 hours, max. It would be good to get away and let your brain recharge, don't you think?"

Jessica began chewing her sandwich again, then swallowed and sipped her coffee. Actually, it would be good. She was back on track now after working late last night, and might be able to squeeze in a quick jaunt up the coast. "You know, that does sound like a good idea," Jessica admitted.

"We'd fly up, of course," Devin said. "No time to drive or take the train, although that would be nice. More restful."

"A change is as good as a rest, or so they say," Jessica quipped. "Although I've yet to experience that. But now I just might? When are we going?" she asked. She brushed a few stray blonde hairs back from her forehead. They'd escaped from the ponytail that she now automatically pulled her hair into each morning, partly because she didn't want to think about it and partly because she didn't have time to wash it.

'Good,' Devin thought. She had already decided that she wanted to go. He wouldn't have to spend the next ten minutes trying to convince her and risking another argument. "In a day or so," he said. "I'm waiting to hear back about the meeting time."

"I think that will work," Jessica replied. "I'm at a good point to pause right now. I'll wrap up a couple of things and set up some work for the staff to handle while I'm away."

Devin leaned over and gave her a quick kiss. "Excellent! And I promise it will take minimal time away from all of this," he said, waving his hand, still holding half a sandwich, toward the bolts of fabric and dress forms scattered around the room.

ଔ

Antonio gargled loudly then spit forcefully into the sink. He took another mouthful of the ghastly lemon and salt concoction and repeated the process, grimacing into the mirror.

"MMMMmmmmmmmmm!!!" he began to hum loudly through his nose, feeling the vibration flow through his nasal passages and into the back of his mouth. "MMmmmooooooooowwwww!" he continued, allowing the vibration to move into his throat.

He put down the glass and walked into the bedroom, still chanting his warm-up exercises. Putting on faded jeans and a black linen shirt, he buttoned it only halfway up so that the gold chain he always wore could be easily seen. He then slipped on soft Italian leather loafers without socks and continued into the living room of his apartment.

Antonio liked to pretend that it was a New York apartment so that he could also pretend that he was preparing for an upcoming performance at the Met. In actuality, it was a reasonably pleasant third-story walkup in Portland and he was part of the local opera and theater company. And his given name was actually Anthony, but *Antonio* sounded much more alluring and operatic.

Now he began his scales. His smooth tenor voice rippled up and down through one scale after another, softly, then loudly, then softly again. Tone and volume were just as important as hitting the right note.

He heard a knock at the door. Good, right on time. He loathed tardiness. Antonio quickly checked his reflection in the mirror by the door, raking his hand through his dark, wavy hair to make it fall over his forehead a bit more in a disheveled manner. He opened the door.

"Hello, Antonio! I could hear you getting started from the hallway!" The woman standing before him was in her sixties with gray hair pulled back into a low bun and glasses that now slipped down her nose. She pushed them back up, a gesture she repeated frequently and unknowingly.

"Good afternoon, my dear Susan!" He said, stepping back and allowing her to enter. "Yes, I'm ready to begin."

"Excellent. I've brought the scores you requested. Where would you like to start?"

Antonio took the sheets of music from her and spread them out on the dining table. "Hmmm," he muttered thoughtfully. "Let's begin here," he said pointing.

Normally, Antonio would have flirted a bit with the woman first, before beginning his work. The age or status of the woman mattered very little to him – he flirted with nearly anyone as it typically enabled him to get his way, often in more ways than one. However, he chose not to flirt with Susan for two reasons. First of all, he needed her unbiased opinion on his singing and flirting would negate that, causing her to overlook flaws or, worse yet in this case, enter into the realm of flattery. It was the nature of flirting. Secondly, he was paying her, and he didn't want to waste his money.

They worked for an hour, Antonio receiving valuable feedback. He was pleased. As he wrote out a check for her fee, she said, "Tell me again what this performance is? Learning just one piece seems unusual."

It was. "It's the opening for an exhibit at the art museum," he said as his pen scribbled along. *"The Costumes of Covent Garden.* Excellent press, for sure," he added. "And the preparation is far less than for an entire show."

Susan agreed. She wished however that it was an entire show. She would have liked to work with him more. His checks always cleared, and she typically had need to cash them promptly. "Very true, with just one piece," she said, trying not to sound disheartened.

He tore the check out and handed it to her. "The only real annoyance is the costume itself. Since that's the whole point of the show, they're going to great pains it seems to make them for the three of us performing. I have a fitting tomorrow that will undoubtedly be endless." He rolled his eyes. "I'm not looking forward to it," he added.

Susan had already put the check in her purse and was heading toward the door. "It's the cross you bear, Antonio," she laughed. "But just think how wonderful you'll look," she said as he reached in front of her for the doorknob. "Not that you need much help in that department!" She couldn't resist a tiny bit of flirting even if he could. She didn't have much excitement in her life these days.

He was unable to resist the complement. "You are too kind! I will invite you to the opening, of course," he said.

Susan now smiled broadly. She patted her hair. "Oh, how wonderful! I wouldn't miss it for the world!" She scurried down the hallway already mentally selecting a dress to wear as he closed the door behind her.

*In opera, as with any performing art,
to be in great demand and to command
high fees you must be good of course,
but you must also be famous.
The two are different things.*

~ Luciano Pavarotti

CHAPTER FOUR

Antonio was already in a foul mood as he strode across the marble floor of the Maine Museum of Art's cavernous foyer. The young man at the front desk had just directed him down the stairs located at the opposite corner from where he had entered. There, evidently, he would meet with someone named Francine and her seamstress who would carry out the fitting of his costume. He had the ridiculous 'visitor' badge clipped to his impeccable silk shirt as he descended the wide staircase. He saw a woman waiting at the bottom.

"You must be Antonio," she said in what sounded to him like an aristocratic accent. That made him feel a tiny bit better. She held out her hand to shake his. "I'm Francine Belmont, Director of Costumes at the Royal Opera."

Antonio's mood changed instantly. The Royal Opera! He hadn't realized someone so high up on the proverbial food chain at Covent Garden would actually be present. He had simply assumed they'd shipped over costumes to be displayed and that someone local would be dressing him. This was certainly a pleasant turn of events!

He smiled his most charming smile broadly, holding out his hand to shake hers. "It's a pleasure to meet you," he said. "Truly an honor to have someone from your esteemed company here!" he added. He was actually being truthful for once. It was an honor, and he hoped it would prove exceedingly helpful for his career. This had gone from a necessary chore to keep his name in the limelight, to almost an audition of sorts. Perhaps things were looking up after all!

"Let me take you down to our makeshift sewing studio," Francine said. "We have everything ready for your fitting."

Antonio's mind was racing. He loved hearing her British accent. He could imagine himself in London, surrounded by people speaking that way. It would be easy for him to adopt it after a while. He had an ear for these things.

He could picture himself onstage at the Royal Opera, singing the best parts. Of course it wouldn't happen immediately, but they would certainly recognize his talent quickly and assign him to increasingly plumb roles.

The smile had not left his face as he followed Francine down the long hallway winding through the storage rooms filled with shrouded sculptures, sturdy wooden crates holding what he assumed were more works of art, and paintings locked behind protective cages. He had never seen the inner workings of an art museum before. Like backstage at an opera house, it was a completely different, haphazard-looking world from the refined and polished public face.

They turned a corner and into one of the many basement rooms lit by small windows high up along the wall. They were at street level and he could hear cars whizzing by. He looked up but saw only the shrubs around the building through the windows.

"Oh, those overlook some private gardens that belong to the museum. Don't worry – no one will be staring in from the street," Francine said as though reading his mind.

Antonio was now annoyed that she'd guessed what he was thinking. "Not at all," he replied smoothly. "I would just hate for anyone to have a preview of your fine work before 'opening night' as it were!"

Francine laughed softly. She knew exactly the sort of person she was dealing with. She had seen his type before, many times. He wasn't going to be able to charm her. However, she'd let him believe he could for a while. It was the easiest way to handle his kind.

In fact, 'his kind' was one of the very reasons she'd chosen to embark on this costume exhibit project in the first place. Her husband had recently left her, taking up with an up-and-coming starlet of the European opera scene. His charming ways had won Francine over a decade prior, but she had slowly come to realize that he was an actor in every aspect of his life. She'd given him ample opportunity to change, overlooking more than one dalliance he'd had, but he had ultimately decided he'd had enough of married life. Francine had loved him, truly, so it hurt when they had parted ways. He had assured her that it was simply his nature to be 'unattached' as he put it so bluntly.

To say that it had come as a shock to Francine that he had so suddenly become 'reattached' and engaged to this young woman would have been an understatement. In reality, it made Francine's blood boil. She felt as though she had wasted over ten years of her life trying to appease him, and all for nothing.

In some ways she felt she had been duped, but Francine knew that you can't dupe someone who knows all the while that it's happening. No, in the end she had only herself to blame. She was thankful she had her work. It made her happy.

Francine refocused, clearing the cobwebs of the past. She was thousands of miles away now, taking on a new venture and really, a new adventure as well. This was her chance to restart.

"This is our head seamstress and my design assistant, Bella Washington," she said, gesturing toward a woman who had just emerged from behind a large rack of clothes.

Antonio stepped forward and quickly shook her hand. "A pleasure," he murmured with only mild enthusiasm. She was not important to him. He wanted to impress Francine.

"I'll leave you to it," Francine said and abruptly left the room.

Now Antonio was visibly annoyed. He had assumed Francine would stay and conduct most of the fitting, simply ordering this meaningless seamstress about. Evidently that was not the case.

"Thank you for coming in," Bella began. "I appreciate your time." She had found that it was best to begin with a somewhat subservient manner, especially with the so-called *divas*, or *divos* as the men would be technically called. No one used the term in common practice, but Bella had heard it once and it stuck in her head. She didn't know anything about him really, but was quite certain after one look that Antonio qualified as a *divo*.

Antonio noticed that she had an American accent. "You're not British," he said flatly.

"No, I'm a New Yorker for the most part," Bella answered, taking a deep-blue coat off a dress form. "I met Francine in New York where I worked for her briefly at the Met, then was hired by the Royal Opera." It was the short version of the story.

"Ah," Antonio replied. He had no time for Bella. She clearly had little influence.

"If we could just slip this on you, I'll see that it fits properly." Bella said, changing the subject.

Antonio turned his back to her and allowed her to slide the coat over his form-fitting silk shirt that encased his shoulders. The coat felt tight in the arms. He was about to mention it when she said, "We'll need to let the arms out a bit. Let's go in front of the mirror and I'll re-pin them."

He walked to the three-way mirror and faced it. She picked up one of his arms and held it out straight, then began removing pins beneath it. She then carefully reinserted the pins in a long row. "Better?" she asked.

Antonio moved his arm around. "Yes, definitely," he replied. "What am I wearing beneath?"

Bella had moved to the other arm. "A simple white silk shirt with a cravat. Most of the shirt won't be seen so we don't have to worry as much about that."

The answer annoyed Antonio. Every bit of his costume mattered, he thought. What if he wanted to remove the jacket at some point during the party? The shirt needed to fit well, to cling to the muscles of his shoulders and arms. He liked to show off all of his assets. "And what about trousers?" he asked.

"We have some generic breeches of standard sizes for men, so those are bound to fit well enough. Francine doesn't want to spend a great deal of effort on these costumes since they'll only be worn for a short period of time. Each of you has only the one song in your performance." She had a pin between her lips as she spoke the last sentence, so the words were mumbled, but he'd heard her well enough.

That was it. Now he was angry. He jerked his arm away, causing Bella to poke him with the pin. He roared as though he'd been stabbed with a knife and tore off the coat. Pins flew everywhere from it. "I will not stand for this!" he shouted. "I am the star tenor and will be treated as such, including receiving a properly fitted costume!" He threw the coat on the floor and marched from the room.

Bella stared, her eyes wide. What had just happened? After a full minute she reached down and picked up the coat. Enough pins were still there so that she could recreate where the seam should be. She carefully put the cerulean fabric back on the dress form and began re-pinning.

"Did I hear something amiss?" It was Francine's voice.

Bella swallowed hard and kept her eyes on her work. She wasn't sure if she was angry or hurt. Or both. She nodded.

"Are you all right?" Francine asked.

Bella took a deep breath. "Yes, just another opera ego to deal with," she finally admitted. "I don't think he liked the fact that we're planning to use off-the-rack trousers."

"But that's common practice, especially for a company performer... Oh! I see," Francine paused, now realizing the problem. "In this troupe, he's a star. Probably quite unused to being treated as an underling. Hmmm!" Francine was nearly laughing now. "Well, nothing wrong with being brought down a peg or two! If he ever wants to reach the big leagues, he'll have to learn that there's a ladder to the top."

Bella had finished her pinning. She turned to her boss. "Yes, there is, and it's pretty steep in places," she replied.

"That it is, Bella. That it is," Francine agreed. "Quite steep. And for our friend Antonio, it may have just become nearly vertical."

The opera world was a very small place. Reputations were everything. Francine knew that it was a lesson Antonio had yet to learn.

ଓ

Dulcie cupped her hands around her eyes and leaned against the window, looking down to the dock below. Bobbing in the late afternoon sun was Dan's boat. She saw him emerge from below deck with what appeared to be a heavy cooler.

"Oh good! Filled with ice already!" she said aloud.

"What's filled with ice?" Rachel had silently sidled up behind her.

Dulcie jumped. "Stop doing that!" she said with mock annoyance.

Rachel grinned. "I can't help it if I'm petite and light on my feet," she said. She leaned toward the window to see what Dulcie was looking at and thumped her head on the glass with a sharp bang. It was so loud that Dan looked up.

"Ow," Rachel said, rubbing her forehead.

"Evidently 'light on one's feet' does not translate to overall grace," Dulcie remarked as she opened the window.

Rachel rolled her eyes.

"Setting things up?" Dulcie yelled down to her brother.

"Yep!" He shouted back. "Never too early to put the bubbly on ice!" he added.

"You got that right!" Dulcie said and pulled her head back in from the window.

"What time are we heading out?" Rachel asked. Dulcie looked at her watch. "In about an hour. Want to go down and see if Bella needs anything? I'm expecting Francine here any minute."

"Aye aye, Cap'n!" Rachel said. She purposefully clomped out of the room so that Dulcie could hear her footsteps. Dulcie snorted in response, then closed the window.

Glancing out one more time, Dulcie saw Nick heading down the dock toward the yacht. He and Dan were becoming fast friends, which made her happy. She had forgiven Nick for making the start of their relationship difficult, but Dulcie had been afraid that her brother wouldn't be quite so understanding. It seemed, however, that he'd managed to get beyond it too. Dulcie exhaled loudly without realizing what she was doing and fogged the window in front of her.

An hour later Dulcie led the small party from the museum down to the gangplank that led to the yacht.

They followed each other in single file as they were welcomed aboard by the captain. Dan had put on a white cotton shirt with the sleeves rolled up, khakis, and his 'dress' boat shoes, as he referred to them. They were exactly like his others, just a bit less worn.

Stepping on the deck, Dulcie let Nick take her arm as he helped steady her. He gave her elbow a quick squeeze, then leaned over for a swift peck on her cheek. "Had to get that in before we were surrounded," he whispered.

Dulcie smiled at him. "Preview of coming attractions, I hope?" she said coyly.

"Play your cards right…," Nick said, trailing off.

Dulcie smacked him softly on the arm, then went over to open the champagne bottles chilling in the cooler.

As she removed the foil and unwound the wire cage from the first bottle, Dulcie watched the others boarding. They were a small party – herself and Nick, Rachel, Francine, Bella, and three others from the Royal Opera company who had been busy pressing the costumes and assisting with the exhibit. They all looked happy to have escaped the basement workrooms of the museum and to be outdoors in the sunshine.

The last person to board was Bella. When Dan turned to assist her down, Dulcie saw him jerk back, as though he had been hit by an unseen force.

Dulcie stopped untwisting the wire that held in the champagne cork as she watched them intently. Bella hadn't noticed anything odd since she was looking down at where she stepped on the steeply angled gangplank. She lost her balance for a moment, and Dan seemed to regain his composure, quickly reaching forward to take her arm and assist her. He must have said something to her, as Dulcie then saw Bella look up at him and smile. She stepped onto the deck and joined the rest of the group.

Dan had his usual deck hand, Freddie, working as first mate, and Dan now left him to untie the yacht and cast off for their trip. As he walked toward the bridge, Dan passed by Dulcie. "What was that all about?" she asked quietly.

"Tell you later," Dan said. He continued up to the bridge and Dulcie heard the yacht's motor start. Soon, they were underway. Dulcie busied herself passing around glasses of champagne. Freddie had secured the lines and now joined Dan on the bridge, who handed over the controls to his assistant so that he could mingle with his passengers.

While she chatted idly with Francine and two of the others, Dulcie saw Dan descending from the bridge. She stepped away from the group as he reached the deck. "So what's up?" she asked pointedly.

Dan wasn't in the mood to pretend that he didn't know what she was talking about. "Who is that woman?" he asked bluntly, nodding in Bella's direction.

Dulcie looked over. "That's Bella Washington. She's the head seamstress and Francine's design assistant. Why?"

Dan swallowed hard. "Ok, I know this is incredibly stupid, especially since it's coming from me, but," he now paused, taking a deep breath. "Do you believe in love at first sight? Because I never have. Until now." He was speaking quickly. "It's like a force came over me. I felt sick and giddy at the same time." Dan glanced at his sister. "All right, stop laughing at me!"

Dulcie forced down the champagne that had nearly bubbled into her nose as she tried not to burst out laughing. "Are you kidding me? Dan Chambers, the confirmed bachelor, never with one woman for longer than a few months…could it be that he's suddenly *in love*?"

"Stop it!" he whispered. "Now I wish I'd never said anything."

"Oh, you'll continue to wish that!" Dulcie said. She was highly amused by this turn of events. "Of course you realize that she lives in London. But you have a boat, so you could just sail over and see her!"

Dan sighed. He knew he'd have to endure more ribbing, for sure. A lot more.

"Well, we'll just have to properly introduce you then, won't we!" Dulcie said. She handed her brother a glass of champagne and steered him across the deck until they reached the young woman. She turned and looked at them as they pointedly approached.

"Hi Bella! Can I introduce, formally, my brother and this vessel's captain, Dan Chambers? Dan, this is Bella Washington."

Dulcie had never seen her brother blush. Nor had she ever seen him at a loss for words. She nearly began laughing again but didn't want to embarrass him, so she quickly continued. "Bella, you're from New York, right?"

Bella nodded but said nothing. Apparently she was tongue-tied as well? Dulcie could see that this was going to be a very one-sided conversation but was determined now. If her brother was suddenly falling in love, it was her mission to ensure he had at least a chance at success. Besides, watching this potential debacle unfold was just too much fun.

"How does London compare?" she asked.

Bella was confused. Why was Dulcie's brother standing there saying nothing, and why was Dulcie so obviously making conversation? Suddenly it dawned on her what was happening. Dan wanted to meet her.

The problem was, she had no interest in meeting him – not as a potential date anyway. She'd never really had anyone in her life, romantically or otherwise, and had learned to live quite contentedly that way. She didn't want to embarrass him though, nor did she want to offend her boss's friend and colleague.

She thought quickly. "I love London," she said. "It's a lot like New York in some ways, but seems more open. Maybe that's because most of the buildings are shorter?" she laughed, trying to lighten the mood.

"Good point!" Dulcie said a bit too enthusiastically. "I never realized that, but you're right!"

"I've only been to each of them briefly," Dan said, apparently finally able to speak. "The cities, I mean. Dulcie is the traveler of the family," he added. He was positive that he sounded incredibly stupid, or at least clumsy.

"The traveler on land, that is," Dulcie corrected him. "Dan's been crew and captain on various boats for years now," Dulcie said. "He's been up and down the East coast and all around the Caribbean."

"Have you ever been across the Atlantic?" Bella asked.

"Twice," Dan said. "Once over to France, then back again."

"What was it like, being so far out that you can't see land?" she asked. She now looked out at the horizon opening up in front of them as they approached the mouth of the harbor.

"Strange, at first," Dan said. "You get used to it after a few days, but initially it feels like you should be able to just turn around and see something other than water."

Bella's shoulders shuddered slightly. "I'm not sure I'd like that." She put her hand on the deck railing as the yacht slowed, powering through the low, rolling swell. "But I do like this," she said. "It's nice to be out here after working in the basement all day."

Dulcie breathed a sigh of relief. Dan appeared to have regained consciousness and some semblance of his former self. She left him to continue his conversation with Bella.

As she turned, Nick approached with a half-empty bottle of champagne. "Need a refill?" he asked.

"Indeed I do!" Dulcie declared.

"And what was that all about?" Nick said quietly as she watched the bubbles foam to the top of her glass while he poured.

Dulcie giggled in spite of herself. "It seems that my esteemed brother, the Ladies Man of all Ladies Men, has a crush. Or, as he put it, it's 'love at first sight'."

Nick choked back a laugh. "Oh, you're kidding!" was all he could manage.

"Nope," Dulcie said. "He was literally speechless when I first introduced him to Bella just now. I've never seen him like that."

"Serves him right for having it so easy all those years. Think it'll go anywhere?" Nick asked as he glanced over at the pair.

"Probably not," Dulcie said. "I mean, she lives in London for one thing, and he doesn't. Plus, I don't get the sense that she's really that interested. It feels like she's just being polite."

"Yet another new situation for your brother!" Nick said. "Well, should be entertaining to see how it all plays out. He'll join the ranks of the rest of us mere mortals."

"That he will," said Dulcie. "Sadly for him, I fear that he will."

If people only knew
how hard I work
to gain my mastery,
it wouldn't seem
so wonderful at all.

~ Michelangelo

CHAPTER FIVE

The small, private plane descended through the cloudless sky and glided down to the runway of Portland jetport. Devin looked over at his wife and smiled. The flight had been a bit extravagant, but he knew it was the only way to convince her to come, as it would mean as little time away from her work as possible. Besides, he could just expense everything since it was, for him, a business trip.

"Steve is picking us up here," Devin said. "He'll drop you off at the hotel on the way over to his office. You can get us checked in, ok?"

Jessica nodded. She was happy to have a little time on her own to regroup, check back in with her staff in New York, and then maybe wander down the streets of Portland. She'd been to the city before, but it had been ages. "Why don't I meet you later at the art museum?" she suggested to her husband.

"Great idea. I'll text you when I'm wrapping up," he said.

Jessica walked down the brick sidewalk that bordered a bumpy, cobblestone street. She'd spent the previous two hours in the hotel room glued to her laptop, focused on the details of her upcoming show. It was good to get outdoors in the sunshine now.

She looked up ahead and saw her husband waiting for her in front of the heavy glass doors of the museum entrance. He waved, and she waved back, quickening her pace.

He gave her a kiss on the cheek when she reached him, then they entered the museum. Devin approached the front desk and spoke quietly to the receptionist. The man nodded, then stepped away from the desk into a hallway behind it.

Moments later, Dulcie accompanied the receptionist to the front desk. "Mr. James! A pleasure to meet you. I got a call from our mutual friend Steve. He said you'd be over." Dulcie reached out, shaking Devin's hand. "This must be your wife the fashion designer?"

Devin nodded proudly as he said, "Yes, this is Jessica James, the next great name in New York fashion," he replied.

Jessica laughed and shook Dulcie's hand as well, saying, "Let's just hope he's right!"

"It's a pleasure to meet you both," Dulcie said. "Steve said that you wanted to see some of the costumes for the upcoming exhibit. Come with me and I'll give you the preview." Dulcie didn't often allow outsiders to view an exhibit before it was finalized, but she made an exception for friends of board members. Especially friends of board members who appeared to be wealthy. Dulcie didn't enjoy this part of the job, pandering to the rich, but at times it was necessary.

She led the couple across the marble floor of the main foyer to a temporary wall that covered the entrance to a closed gallery. They could hear a drill running and a hammer tapping as softly as possible, the sounds of several workers behind the wall who were busy assembling the new exhibit. Dulcie carefully pulled the small door in the wall open and they slipped through.

One of the workers looked up, and Dulcie gave him a half wave. He nodded, smiled, and looked back down again, firing up his drill. It appeared that they were building tiny wooden platforms.

"The exhibit will be in here, but I'm afraid we're a little behind schedule," Dulcie said. "Most of the costumes will be on mannequins that are being placed on these little platforms. However, the mannequins have been delayed, so we're scrambling to make some temporary arrangements in the meantime. Nothing like last minute snafus, right?" Dulcie laughed.

Jessica nodded. "Yes, I'm hoping for as few of those as possible," she said.

"When is your show?" Dulcie asked. The board member had said that Jessica was putting together her first collection to launch herself as a designer.

"In a little over a week," Jessica answered.

"Nearly there!" Devin added, with a mock mopping of his brow. Jessica elbowed him playfully.

"This is the boring bit for you then," Dulcie said as she gestured toward the construction area. "It's the costumes you've come to see." She led the way across the room, then opened a back door almost completely hidden in a corner. They descended a winding narrow stairway that entered onto a decidedly unglamorous long basement hallway. Wooden crates lined the wall on one side. Jessica noted they were all labeled with the stenciled words, 'Royal Opera, Covent Garden,' and she felt a shiver run up her spine.

They turned and entered a large room with sunlight streaming in from windows near the ceiling. Rolling garment racks were everywhere, filled with elaborate costumes from multiple performances. Two workers stood in a corner, leaning over a steamer and an ironing board, removing wrinkles from a garment that had just been taken out of a nearby crate.

"And here we are," Dulcie said. "The somewhat unglamourous side to any show, be it onstage or otherwise!" she gestured around her.

As she did, she saw Bella making her way around the racks of clothes. When she emerged at last, Bella stopped quickly. "*Jessica?*" she exclaimed. "What on Earth are you doing here?" she said, smiling.

Jessica turned and inhaled sharply. "*Bella!*" she nearly shouted, running over and hugging the young woman. "How long has it been?" she asked rhetorically, then turned to her husband and Dulcie. "We went to design school together!" she explained to both of them.

Bella nodded. "I'd heard you were still in New York," she said.

"And I'd heard you weren't, but wasn't sure where you'd gone! I had no idea it was as exciting as this!" Jessica waved her arm at the colorful racks filling the room.

"But I've forgotten my manners. This is my husband Devin," she said as he extended his hand to Bella. "And Devin, this is my classmate Bella." Jessica turned back to her friend. "As you can see, I got married since leaving college," she added unnecessarily and grinned.

"Good for you!" Bella replied. "Are you still designing?"

Jessica nodded, and Devin quickly said, "She's quite brilliant, and has her first collection showing soon!"

"That's fabulous!" Bella said. "I'd love to see it if I can. All of this is keeping me busy right now, though," she said. But you'll have the pictures online probably, right? You've got a website, yes?"

Jessica nodded happily. "It's all coming. I can't post anything yet from the collection as I don't want to ruin the surprise before the show."

"Of course not," Bella replied. "But I can't wait to see it." She looked over at Dulcie. "In the meantime, I'm assuming you're here to see what's going to be displayed in the costume exhibit?"

"Yes," Dulcie replied. "And if you have a few moments, could I leave our guests with you, Bella? I have to speak with Francine next door. I'll be right back," Dulcie said. Bella nodded and as Dulcie left she could already hear them chatting about the fabrics and designs.

When Dulcie returned, the former classmates were in deep discussion about a particular sewing technique they had both learned. Devin stepped over to Dulcie. "I'm glad to get my wife out of her own studio for a while," he said. "She's been working nonstop for too long."

"Sounds like the curse of a perfectionist," Dulcie said.

"That it is," Devin agreed. "But she and I share that trait, so I can understand," he added.

Dulcie turned to him. "Steve mentioned on the phone that you were in town on business? Are you in the same line as he is?" She knew that Steve's public relations firm had been expanding rapidly in the past few years."

"I have a marketing firm in New York, so our work goes hand in hand. We've paired up on a couple of contracts in the past, and I wanted to talk to him about a new venture. The timing worked out well all around," he said looking back over at his wife.

"I'm glad it did," Dulcie said. "But you can't stay longer for the exhibit opening?" she asked.

"I'm afraid not," Devin replied. "Jessica can only spare this one overnight trip. She insists she needs to get back tomorrow."

"I know what it's like to be in the middle of a project," Dulcie laughed.

"Yes, and we shouldn't take up any more of your time either," Devin said. Jessica and Bella had finished their discussion and rejoined them.

"This is heaven!" Jessica announced. "Thank you, all of you, for showing me around and letting me ask too many questions!"

Bella smiled. "I'm happy to share all this. It's great to see you again!" She was beginning to feel anxious and wanted to get back to her work. The exhibit opening was in only two days and they had far too much left to finish.

"You too, Bella! I'll send you an invitation to my show. I hope you can make it, but if you can't let me know what you think of my work from the website, ok?" Jessica said.

"Absolutely!" Bella replied. She gave her friend a quick hug and waved as they left.

Once they were gone, Bella turned and disappeared behind the garment racks She let her hands trail along the yards and yards of ornate fabrics until she found the one that she wanted to touch the most: the cerulean velvet. She buried her arms into it, hugging it close to her and closing her eyes as she did.

∞

'They're here!'

Dulcie glanced down at the text that had just come through on her phone. *'Who is here?'* she thought with some alarm. She wasn't expecting anyone and frankly didn't have any more time to spare for visitors. Then it dawned on her; the text was from Rachel. It must be the mannequins.

'Loading dock?' Dulcie texted back.

Rachel sent her back a thumbs-up emoji.

Dulcie hurried down the stairs and through the winding basement corridors to the back of the building. She could already hear a truck beeping as it backed up. She rounded the corner past the security office and blinked several times.

The entire dock area was flooded with sunlight. The huge overhead doors covering the loading dock bay had been thrown open and the truck driver was now noisily unfastening the doors of the trailer. They creaked loudly on their hinges as she pushed them aside.

"Delivery for a D. Chambers!" the driver announced. "Looks like a party in there," she added, pointing to the mannequins carefully wrapped before they had been wedged into the space.

Dulcie stepped forward and signed the clipboard the driver now handed to her. The building staff was ready, unloading the human forms more gently than Dulcie had seen them carry some of the priceless artworks. She wasn't sure if that was because she was standing there watching, or if somehow these blobs of plastic and metal seemed alive to them and therefore required more care.

Rachel scurried around with her own clipboard, counting the mannequins and making sure there were the correct numbers to match the order she had put in. When the last one had been placed on the loading dock she turned to Dulcie. "Question. Will Francine and Bella and the crew dress them downstairs then move them up, or just put the costumes on them upstairs in the gallery?" she asked.

Dulcie thought for a moment. The staff that had just unloaded the mannequins were now arranging them in little groups as though they were chatting with each other at an awkward cocktail party. Dulcie chuckled at their antics.

Turning back to Rachel she said, "Probably downstairs. They can go up in the freight elevator once they're dressed, then they can put the finishing touches on with the proper lighting upstairs. Otherwise, Francine would have to move their whole operation up to the gallery, and I don't think she'd want to do that."

Rachel nodded. "I'll alert the troops," she said.

A raucous laugh erupted from across the room. "Hey, Rachel!" the foreman called over as she approached them. "Tommy just asked this one out!" Rachel shook her head, glancing back at Dulcie and rolling her eyes.

Dulcie left them and went down the corridor toward the room she'd last spotted Francine in. She poked her head around the corner. Francine was kneeling on the floor alongside Bella, engrossed in a hem.

"I've got some good news," Dulcie announced. "The mannequins are coming, the mannequins are coming!" she said in her best Paul Revere voice.

"Oh, exciting!" Francine declared. "When?"

At that moment they heard voices in the hallway. "Right now," Dulcie replied. "I assumed you'd want to dress them down here, then move them up. Is that correct?"

"Oh, yes," Francine said. "Absolutely!" She stepped into the hallway. "Let's put several in each room here and we'll take it from there," she added. "Could we leave some in the hallway?" she asked Dulcie.

"I don't see why not," Dulcie answered.

Bella had now finished the hem and joined them. She breathed a sigh of relief. This was the final step toward completion of the exhibit. Although no one had said anything aloud, they had all been concerned that there wouldn't be enough time to dress the mannequins or, worse yet, they wouldn't appear in time at all. It would be a push to complete everything before the opening, but Bella had worked around the clock before to prepare for a performance. It was part of the job.

"Bella, are we done with the fittings for the performers?" Francine asked, jarring Bella from her thoughts.

"Nearly," she responded. "I have a final one tomorrow with the tenor." She'd been putting it off, given their last encounter, but had no choice now. She just hoped that everything would fit perfectly and no further alterations would be needed. It would minimize her time with Antonio and his attitude.

"Good," said Francine. "This feels like the final preparation before opening night, doesn't it?" she said.

Bella nodded. Indeed it did. Always the final time crunch. Always the little details. Always the difficult diva or divo, as the case may be. It felt very much like the mad push before opening night.

℃

Dan helped the last passenger up onto the gangplank and watched carefully, making sure that everyone safely reached the dock and continued along toward the street.

He turned back to see the late afternoon sunshine sparkle on the water. The boat rose and fell softly beneath him, calming his mind. He had been on edge lately, an uncharacteristic feeling. Why?

He knew the catalyst was Bella. She had sparked something in him that he'd been ignoring for quite some time. His life had always been carefree, a few setbacks here and there, but mostly following a live-and-let-live kind of philosophy. Each day was a fresh new beginning.

Now, however, he found his mind wandering into the future. His future. And sharing that future. Maybe it was the investment in the yacht and setting up the company. He and Dulcie were partners in it, using the inheritance that she'd unexpectedly received. She was a silent partner though, and the actual day-to-day work was left up to him. It was a good arrangement for both of them.

Dan knew that his change in attitude could also be simply age. As he grew older, he realized life was more fragile. He wouldn't admit it to himself fully, but the thought frightened him. He found himself sometimes waking up in the morning wishing he could see a familiar face beside him. And since Bella had first stepped onto the deck, it was her face, oddly beautiful, ethereal, that he wanted to see.

A motion caught his eye across the water. As if the universe had read his mind, he saw Bella standing at one of the museum windows. He knew she was upstairs in Dulcie's office. He heard his breath catch and without realizing it, put his hand up to his chest. His heart was beating rapidly.

Was this what truly being in love felt like? It was as though he was excruciatingly happy and horribly sick at the same time. He sat down and closed his eyes for a moment.

When he opened them again, she was gone.

When in doubt, wear red.

~ Bill Blass

CHAPTER SIX

"Have you ever felt rested before an opening event?" Rachel already knew the answer before asking the question.

Dulcie's eyes did not leave her laptop screen. "I don't have enough energy to answer that," she replied. Closing the computer abruptly she said, "I need coffee. Badly."

"And I need a pen that writes," Rachel said, shaking the pen that she held vigorously, hoping that would help.

Dulcie reached into her desk drawer, pulled out a pen, and tossed it over to Rachel. Then she stood up and stretched her back. "Want a coffee too?" she asked.

Rachel scribbled something on the clipboard which had now become an extension of her arm and clicked the pen closed. "Thanks, but I'll come with you," she said. "I need to see how things are going with the setup."

Rachel bounced out the door. Dulcie noticed that she was wearing ballet flats with springy soles and wished she had done the same. Her heels weren't exactly high today, but she knew she would be aching from her higher pumps when she put them on later.

It had already been a long day and wasn't getting any shorter. They'd managed to get most of the clothed mannequins upstairs, deciding at the last minute to leave a few out in order to focus on making the rest perfect. Francine had made that call after learning that Bella had the final fitting with the Terrible Tenor, as they had taken to calling him. It was of course said with a French accent for effect, in spite of his Italian name. Dulcie had yet to meet him but already disliked him.

With a coffee mug firmly planted in her palm, Dulcie now followed Rachel into one of the basement workrooms. Bella was readying herself for Antonio's appearance.

"You up for this?" Rachel asked.

Bella inhaled deeply and sighed. "No choice. Maybe he'll be fine. Sometimes they tend to be a bit more cooperative on game day," she said. "I've wondered from time to time if they've self-medicated," she added. "Once I had to sew a special pocket into a pair of costume trousers for a flask. And it wasn't a prop for the character he was playing!"

Dulcie laughed and was about to reply when the subject of Bella's musing appeared at the door. Dulcie stepped forward, knowing who he was instantly. She held out her hand to shake his as she said, "You must be our illustrious tenor! I'm thrilled to meet you. I'm Dr. Chambers."

Rachel turned away to hide her smirk. Dulcie never used her title unless she was asserting her authority. It was a subtle but affective device.

"Ah yes, and it's a pleasure to meet you as well," Antonio replied, clearly enjoying having his ego stroked. "I'm looking forward to this evening," he added. "Will all of you be there?"

"Yes, of course," Dulcie replied. She noticed the hint of an Italian accent although she knew full well that he was from Boston and not Italy. Being fluent in Italian herself Dulcie wondered what his reaction would be if she began speaking that language rather than English. For Bella's sake, however, she decided to let it go. Better to have him in a good mood for the fitting after what she'd been told happened the last time. She turned to Rachel. "We should get on with checking things upstairs and leave them to it. I'm sure Antonio," she pronounced it in the Italian manner, "Is very busy today and I know we are!" She smiled winningly at him as she thanked him for coming in, then left.

Bella quickly grabbed the beautiful blue coat and slipped it on Antonio. He preened in front of the three-way mirror, spinning about and twisting to see every angle. "Yes, it is quite perfect," he declared at last. Bella nodded in agreement. So far she had not uttered a word. "Am I to also try on the shirt and pants?" he added as he removed the coat.

Bella had the other garments ready knowing that Antonio would want to make sure that they fit perfectly. She began to gesture toward a screen in the corner when Antonio suddenly stripped off his shirt. Bella quickly handed him the shirt from the costume. He slipped it over each shoulder, then simply stood in front of her with arms out, shirt gaping and chest exposed, waiting for her to button it.

Bella had worked with many performers, including quite a few flirtatious ones, but had yet to feel this uncomfortable. He had been rude and arrogant to her the first time she had met him, and now it seemed that he was being suggestive? Or perhaps she was just interpreting things the wrong way. She was tired, and certainly apprehensive about working with him.

He saw her hesitate and dropped his arms. Reaching down he quickly unzipped his jeans and let them fall to the floor, stepping out of them and his leather loafers at the same time. He now stood barefoot and nearly naked in front of Bella, save for the fully open silk shirt and his tight underwear that left nothing to the imagination. Bella glanced toward the door and noted that it was open, feeling relieved.

Antonio had followed her glance and also realized that anyone could walk in at any moment. He simply shrugged at her, gave her a smile that bordered onto a sneer, then took the britches that she handed him and put them on. He then buttoned the shirt himself, tucking it into the waist of the pants. He looked at his reflection in the mirror.

"These fit quite well," he said. "I am surprised." It was a mild condescension that was not lost on Bella. She took several steps back.

"You are done, then," she finally said. "You can leave the garments over the screen when you change," she added, pointing again to the screen in the corner of the room. "Thank you for coming in," she ended the conversation abruptly and left the room, darting through the hallway and into the next room where she could hear others talking as they worked.

Antonio reached down and picked up his own garments and slipped behind the screen. He quickly put on his jeans and shirt again and slid on the soft leather loafers. He carefully hung the costume back up, not because had any respect for Bella's work, but simply because he knew he'd be wearing it that evening. He then sauntered from the room.

❦

As usual, Dulcie had no time to go home and properly change before the opening event. She'd grown used to getting dressed in her office and had even brought her evening clothes in with her that morning knowing full well that she would run out of time. However, she did allow herself the indulgence of a glass of champagne while she got dressed and did her hair and makeup. It was a necessary 'attitude adjustment' she believed. Besides, she loved champagne and it was as good an excuse as any.

Her attire this evening was a simple, black long-sleeved but off-the-shoulder dress with a full knee-length skirt. She pulled her dark hair back into a chignon as she did for nearly every opening, adding a few sparkling rhinestone pins to brighten it up and keep it in place. A simple gold chain and diamond stud earrings complemented the hairpins. The only pizzazz in the look was a pair of subtle black and white snakeskin pumps. She'd debated over whether to wear them or just the plain black ones, but decided in the end that the snakeskin was more fun. This was all about costumes and opera, after all, where 'over the top' was not even in the vocabulary.

Flicking on some extra mascara, Dulcie looked at her reflection in the full-length mirror one more time and nodded. Good enough. She strode across the room, unlocked her office door and pulled it open just as Nick was about to knock. He stepped back and stared for a moment.

"Wow, Dulcie! You look fantastic!" He swept an arm around her waist and planted a kiss on her lips. "Sorry, couldn't stop myself!" he said.

Dulcie giggled. He had a way of making her feel amazing regardless of how she looked, but in this particular case, she knew she did look quite good. "You flatter me, sir!" she replied coyly.

"Very true and very warranted," he said. "Now, what can I do to help?" Nick knew that in spite of the festive atmosphere and attire, Dulcie was in work mode.

"One thing you could do is track down Dan to see if he's made it here yet. He's my unofficial greeter, per usual. Folks should be arriving soon so I'd love it if he was somewhere near the door."

"I'm on it," Nick said. He winked at her and left in search of her brother. Nick knew that Dulcie was an introvert and had to work hard at these events to socialize. It was the one part of her job that she despised. Dan, on the other hand, was the extrovert, expert at schmoozing, chatting, and otherwise being the social butterfly. It was lucky for Dulcie that he was almost always available for such events. But then, Nick thought, maybe she had helped him out with setting up his company for that very reason – so Dan would be nearby to help her as well. It was a case of sibling symbiosis, perhaps.

Dan had just entered the front door as Nick walked by the reception desk. He gave him a friendly punch on the shoulder. Dan smiled, but Nick noticed he looked distracted. In his line of work as a detective, Nick had learned to size up people quickly. Dan now lacked the easygoing nature he usually seemed to exude. "What's up?" he said. "Everything ok?"

Dan tried to smile reassuringly. "Yeah, yeah. Just not feeling my normal self this evening," he said distractedly.

"Well I have a message from the boss that she needs you near the door. Want a glass of something to clear your head? Or muddle it properly, as the case may be?" Nick tried to keep his tone light.

"That'd be great," Dan said. "Scotch on the rocks would be perfect."

"Coming right up," Nick replied over his shoulder as he headed toward the bar set up in the corner. As he ordered the drink and included another for himself, he thought it was odd. Out of character. Dan typically avoided the hard liquor and had a champagne or even just a beer at these events. Nick knew that Dan realized they were not just social gatherings, but important to Dulcie's work as well as his own. Portland was a small place and connections, in any line of work, were important.

He brought the drinks back over and clinked his glass against Dan's. As Dan sipped his scotch, Nick saw him flinch as he looked across the rapidly filling room. Glancing over, Nick noticed that Bella had just appeared. She looked radiant in a form-fitting wine colored dress that made her dark skin appear to glow. Her hair was braided into a simple plait that fell down the back of her slender neck. Her eyes seemed to glimmer although Nick could not quite determine how or why.

Dan was clearly shellshocked, unable to speak or even move. "You gonna ask her out?" Nick asked.

Dan broke off his gaze and looked at the floor, then took a gulp of his drink. "I already did," he answered. He didn't need to say anything else. The look on his face was enough. Bella had turned him down.

"Sorry, man," Nick murmured. "And I know you're not used to the ladies saying no." He tried to say it in a joking manner, but realized as soon as the words came out that Dan was hurt.

"No, I'm not," he replied curtly. "And this was different." He now drained his glass. "I need a refill," he said and abruptly walked away.

Nick stared after him.

"What the heck was that?" The gravelly voice behind Nick made him jump. His partner at the Portland Police, Detective Adam Johnson had slid up behind him, no mean feat given that the man was quite large. Nick was always surprised at how agile he could be.

"I think that our friend Mr. Chambers has experienced heartbreak for the first time in his life," Nick said.

Johnson nodded. "Ah, yes. He's now joined us in the ranks of mere mortals."

"Had to happen someday," Nick agreed. "Hey, we're not here on official business now, are we?" Johnson wasn't known for attending social events, especially more formal ones, so his presence was unusual. He wasn't a fan of 'looking like a penguin' as he put it although Nick had yet to see him actually in a tux. The thought of it made him laugh.

"What, you think I can't hold my own with the hoity toity?" Johnson mocked. "Dulcie invited me and the missus. She likes opera singing so I figured it was a good outing."

Nick nodded. Johnson's wife was a tiny Italian woman and Nick knew Adam adored her. If she wanted to hear opera, Johnson would take her to hear opera. Of course this particular evening had the advantage of just a small dose of arias, not an entire evening filled with it. Johnson was well aware of that fact, much to his own relief. He was also aware that there would be a hearty supply of snacks.

Johnson spotted Dulcie emerging from the back offices. "There's your dream girl," he said. Nick just grinned.

Dulcie approached and gave Johnson a quick hug. "Love the shoes," he said.

"Oh god, me too!" Dulcie admitted. "I took a preemptive Tylenol just so I could wear them. Totally worth it."

"Agreed," Johnson said.

Dulcie glanced around the room. "All right, I'd love to chat with you boys but it's off to the races for me now," she said, changing the subject. "Wish me luck."

The two men raised their glasses in response.

Dulcie went over to the platform that had been set up at the back of the room. It contained a table and chair – props for the singers – as well as a microphone positioned in the center. Dulcie stepped up and switched on the microphone. She tried to hide her unsteadiness. Somehow, she was always nervous speaking at these events. She would never get used to having the spotlight on herself.

She acknowledged and thanked the musicians that had been playing the pieces from various operas while the guests mingled and would now accompany the singers. The soprano would now begin the formal entertainment with the famous habanera from *Carmen*. Dulcie introduced her, then stepped off the stage.

The moment the singer was in the bright lights, she seemed to actually become her character. Her gypsy dress, red of course, was an exquisite combination of satin and Spanish lace. She had a brightly patterned shawl with long fringe draped over her shoulders that she flipped about as she sang the provocative aria. Her black lace mantilla had black crystals sewn into it, making her dark hair sparkle. A single red rose appeared to hold the mantilla in place.

Francine had joined Dulcie in the shadows to the side of the stage. " 'Love is a rebellious bird'," she leaned over and whispered, translating from the French libretto. "It was quite a scandalous part when it first premiered back in the 19th century," she added.

"If they could only see what's on television today!" Dulcie whispered back. Francine stifled a giggle. Dulcie scanned the audience, most standing with cocktails still in hand, a few of the older guests sitting on benches that had been scattered around the space. The turnout had been good, most likely because this opening had such interesting entertainment.

As Carmen concluded her piece and curtsied to the applause, Dulcie stepped onto the stage and thanked her, then introduced their next performer. This was Figaro from *The Barber of Seville*, singing *Largo al factotum*. It was a perennial favorite of course with the repeating "Figaro, Figaro…Figaro, Figaro…!" verses.

The baritone was a brilliant comic actor as well, strutting up and down the stage emphasizing his own self-importance. His white linen shirt was haphazardly tucked into broadly striped pants giving him a clownlike appearance. The unbuttoned vest, sewn of a crushed velvet that matched the burgundy stripe of the pants, also portrayed him as a hard-working and busy man.

Dulcie turned to Francine during the song and said, "Love the pants!"

Francine grinned. "Fun to design," she whispered back. "Figaro is a clever liar but a moral person overall. We get a lot of latitude dressing him."

Dulcie reminded herself, once again, that costume design, like every other kind of art, was a form of communication. Clothes weren't simply something to be worn, they conveyed a message. On stage, that was a critical part of the character.

Figaro concluded to roaring laughter and, as he made his final bow, he helped Dulcie back up onto the platform, kissing her hand as he did. The audience laughed again.

"My goodness!" Dulcie said into the microphone. "He'll also be giving haircuts later if anyone is interested," she joked. She then introduced the final performance. This was Antonio singing the beautiful *Nessun dorma* from *Turandot*. It was intended to be the highlight of the evening as the aria, if performed well, could bring the house down.

Dulcie left the stage and Antonio stepped forward as the strains from the violin began. He did not disappoint. He may have been lacking in other respects, Dulcie thought, but the man could certainly sing.

"Unrequited love for the beautiful Turandot, and yet he persists," Francine whispered about his character

Calaf. The colors in Antonio's cerulean coat seemed to shift from dark to light and every variation in between as he subtly moved while the music rose and fell. Dulcie found herself admiring Bella's work – the coat fit him perfectly, allowing him to move without it appearing to stretch or pull, yet it never looked too loose or too tight. How Bella could tailor it so precisely, and in such a short amount of time, was a marvel.

As the the song's conclusion began to build, chills ran down Dulcie's spine. Antonio reached the final, triumphant notes and extended them for as long as possible, as was now expected since Pavarotti had popularized the song.

The audience simply erupted when Antonio finished. Cheers of "Bravo!" rang out. Antonio continued to bow and bask in the accolades. Dulcie then heard someone shout "Encore!" and decided that it was time to bring the evening's entertainment to a conclusion. No one had rehearsed an additional piece, and Dulcie did not want to further encourage Antonio.

She stepped onstage and quickly thanked him, seeing the annoyance in his eyes as he had been effectively cut off, then she thanked the other performers by name once again. She then introduced Francine who expressed her thanks to everyone as well.

When the performance was over, Francine hugged Dulcie. "A huge success!" she announced. "Dulcie, I can't thank you enough!"

"Francine, I'm thrilled! And everyone has been raving about the costumes as well. You've pulled it off!"

"*We've* pulled it off!" Francine said. "Now I must find Bella and congratulate her. She's worked so hard on all of this and deserves credit!"

She hurried off as Dulcie located Nick in the crowd. Most of the guests had now begun to drift off, some more tipsy than others. Dulcie was glad that they'd set up velvet ropes a good distance away from the exhibit pieces. The last thing that she needed was a stray glass of champagne splashed on an expensive silk gown. Dulcie motioned to Nick with a sideways jerk of the head that she was heading to her office. She saw him politely extract himself from his conversation and knew he would join her.

He did, but not without first digging deep into the cooler behind the bar to find the bottle of Veuve Clicquot buried at the bottom. It was a long tradition, to hide a bottle there during the event, then pop the cork when the guests had departed. She had learned it from her old friend and mentor who had held Dulcie's position as museum director before her. Dulcie grinned as Nick entered with the bottle and two glasses.

"Quite an evening!" he said as he pried off the foil, then the cork's cage.

"I'll say!" Dulcie agreed. "I believe 'without a hitch' is the phrase," she added.

Nick poured the bubbles carefully and handed her a glass. They clinked them together. "To yet another success," he said.

"Yet another!" Dulcie echoed.

Nick sat down in the chair opposite her desk. "Not to put a damper on things, but your brother seemed a little off."

Dulcie frowned for a moment. "Yes, I don't think it's gone well for him with Bella."

"I know for a fact that it hasn't," Nick informed her. "He evidently asked her out this evening, but she turned him down."

"Wow, that's probably a first for Dan!" Dulcie said.

The musicians had packed up and the museum was growing quiet. Dulcie glanced out the window and saw the lights on in Dan's yacht. She was surprised. He usually stopped by her office following an event and shared a glass of 'the good stuff' is he liked to call it. She then saw the control panel lights on the bridge come on and heard the boat's motor start.

"What the heck…?" Dulcie said, going over to the window. She opened it to see the yacht nosing out of its slip and heading out into the darkness toward the harbor.

"What's he doing?" Nick asked, now standing beside her.

"I have no idea," Dulcie said.

"I know he had a couple of scotches tonight. He usually doesn't have the hard stuff at these things – just sticks to beer or champagne. Should I contact the harbormaster?" Nick asked.

Dulcie thought for a moment. She knew her brother wouldn't do anything deliberately dangerous. He knew the water too well. "Let me call him first." She grabbed her cellphone. Dan didn't answer so she left a message.

Then she sent a text asking if he was all right. He didn't respond.

"I'm going to go out and see if Johnson is still around," Nick said, already in the doorway. "Maybe he knows something?"

Dulcie nodded, still staring at her phone, willing it to come to life with a message from her brother. This was so unlike him.

Nick had only been gone a moment when Francine raced in, breathless. "I can't find Bella," she said. "I'm a bit worried because we'd agreed to go back to the hotel together. I doubt she'd have gone without at least contacting me first. I just called her cell phone but she didn't answer."

Dulcie's brow furrowed. This was all too strange. First Dan and now Bella? "Maybe she's still downstairs?" she said.

"I just looked, but I'd be happy to go down there again," Francine said.

"Yes, I'm sure she's around," Dulcie replied. She didn't mention Dan's odd behavior. Could he and Bella have gone off on the boat together? Given the evening's events it didn't seem likely.

Dulcie grabbed her phone in case Dan called back, and followed Francine downstairs. Most of the lights had been turned off and the streetlights from outdoors cast an eerie glow through the small windows high up in the rooms. Several mannequins were still in the dark hallway, lined up against the wall in various poses. Their shadows looked ominous. When Dulcie reached the first panel of light switches she quickly hit them all at once. The room flooded with light. Both she and Francine now squinted in the glare.

They called out Bella's name but heard nothing. Dulcie walked in between the garment racks, now mostly empty. She stepped over some remnants of fabrics, carful not to slip as she was still wearing her high-heeled pumps.

Dulcie glanced at her phone, then turned back to Francine. "What's Bella's cell phone number?" she asked. Francine told her and Dulcie dialed.

They both froze, silent. Then they heard the distant sound of a phone ringing. It was in the next room. They hurried in and Dulcie quickly flipped on the light switches.

Lying all but hidden in a corner amongst several bolts of fabrics that were twisted around her was Bella. She was motionless.

Dulcie raced over and saw what looked like an EpiPen in Bella's right hand. She was still wearing her cocktail dress and heels, as though she had just come downstairs from the party.

Dulcie reached down to check her pulse but already knew the answer. Bella was dead.

Color helps to express light –
not the physical phenomenon,
but the only light that really
exists, that in the artist's brain.

~ Henri Matisse

CHAPTER SEVEN

Nick had located his partner upstairs in the museum, polishing off a plate of hors d'oeuvres. Nick was about to tell Johnson about Dan and his odd behavior with the yacht when his phone rang. It was Dulcie. Maybe she'd heard from her brother?

"Dulcie, did he call back?" Nick asked.

"Come downstairs now, please," Dulcie said, ignoring his question. "Is Johnson there?"

"Yes," Nick said. He knew now that something was very wrong.

"Can his wife get home on her own?" Dulcie asked.

"Probably," Nick replied. "Be right there."

Moments later Dulcie met Nick at the bottom of the stairs. "What's going on?" he said.

"Bella is dead," she told him bluntly.

"Oh my god," Nick said softly. He knew they were both thinking about Dan's sudden departure.

They hurried into the workroom where Francine was still standing over Bella's body. Francine was crying now, shaking her head. Dulcie put her arms around her friend and coaxed her out of the room, into the hallway. Johnson came barreling down the stairs but stopped when he saw Francine.

"Nick's in there," Dulcie pointed.

Johnson went in and joined his partner who was already surveying the scene.

"Should I call forensics?" Johnson asked. "Foul play, or just a tragic accident?"

"I don't know," Nick replied. "At first glance, looks like an accident. Anaphylaxis, I think. She used an EpiPen," he pointed to her hand and the spot on her thigh where it looked like the injection had taken place. "I don't think it was enough to save her."

"Damn," Johnson muttered. "Bad luck. Horrible." He looked more closely at her face. "Yup, swelling around the eyes and mouth. Looks like she was allergic to something," he said.

"Agreed," Nick said. "I'll call forensics and get the team over here," he said. He turned away, and Johnson could hear him speaking quietly on the phone.

Johnson went back into the hallway where Dulcie was still with Francine. "It looks like anaphylactic shock.

Was she allergic to anything that you were aware of?" he asked Francine.

She wiped her eyes with a now-soggy tissue. "I know she had a nut allergy. But she was always very careful. She never ate anything from sources she didn't know, and usually carried her own food. Plus she always had two EpiPens in her purse."

"We only see the one, but the other could have been dropped somewhere. Do you know where she kept her purse while she was in the building?" Johnson asked.

"Usually in the lower cupboard, on the far side of the room."

Johnson thanked her and went back into the workroom just as Nick ended his call. "Should be two pens," Johnson said. "She kept them in her purse." He started opening cupboard doors until he found the purse. He rummaged through it. "Nope, not in here. Must be on the floor somewhere," he said.

The two men dropped down to their hands and knees and began crawling around on the floor. Nick finally located it, under a rolling garment rack. "That mystery is solved," he said. "But we don't know what triggered the reaction."

"Forensics can tell us that," Johnson grunted as he struggled to stand up again.

"Here's something strange though. If she obviously was having a sudden reaction, one that was extreme enough for her to know she'd need both pens, why would she take them out of her purse, then close it and put it back in the cupboard? If your face and throat are swelling up, don't you just grab what you need and drop everything else, literally?"

Johnson stared at the purse for a moment. "Yeah, that is weird," he finally said. "Maybe habit to toss it back in the cupboard? Maybe she wasn't sure if she was going to use the pens?"

"Not very likely," Nick replied.

"Still, if you're not thinking straight…," Johnson said. He liked to consider all possibilities.

They heard a commotion beyond the room out in the hallway. The forensics team had arrived. Dulcie was glad that Nick had had the foresight to tell them to come around to the back of the building and in by the loading dock. It would be easier to access the room, and would also draw less attention. It wasn't even ten o'clock yet and Dulcie didn't want to have to explain this to the news outlets, or her own board members for that matter, any sooner than necessary.

Truth be told, she could barely explain it to herself right now.

❧

Dulcie woke to the sound of her cellphone buzzing on the nightstand. She'd managed to get Francine back to her hotel the night before, and had explained what she could to Rachel who was also visibly shaken. She and Bella were becoming fast friends.

Nearly knocking the phone on the floor as she reached for it, Dulcie saw that it was Nick. "Hi, I'm awake," she said.

"Just barely, it sounds like," he replied.

"MmmmHmm," she answered, rubbing her eyes.

"Mind if I come around for coffee?" he asked.

"Ok. Yes. Sure,' she said, "But only if you're making it."

"I'll do one better," he said. "I'll bring it."

"You're a saint," Dulcie replied.

"That's what they all say," Nick quipped and clicked off the phone.

Dulcie got up, wrapped herself in her robe, located her slippers and padded into the bathroom. She washed her face, brushed her teeth and attempted to make her hair look moderately un-slept-in. Not that it would matter since Nick knew she'd been asleep.

Dulcie heard a knock on the door. She opened it and Nick came in carrying two large cardboard cups with plastic covers and a white paper bag. "That's something delicious which I don't need but want anyway, right?" Dulcie said taking one of the coffees and pointing to the bag. Nick just laughed and handed it to her. She peeked in. Blueberry muffins. "You *are* a saint," she said.

"You mentioned that before," he replied and sat down at the table.

Dulcie joined him, then popped up and scurried into the kitchen for napkins. "So do we know anything yet from forensics?" she asked as she sat down again. Her stomach growled. She realized that she hadn't had dinner the night before and tore open the bag. Nick smiled in spite of himself. He was glad Dulcie wasn't the type to pretend she didn't have an appetite.

Nick made himself refocus on their current problem. He frowned now, thinking about the events that had transpired the night before. "We don't know much yet, only that it appears to be a nut allergy as Francine had thought. They think peanuts. Not uncommon at all. Lots of crackers and breads and things can be contaminated at a factory where peanut things have been made. We'll need to check with the caterer to see who their suppliers are."

"Do we know yet what she ate?" Dulcie asked.

"Nope. Lots of tests to do still," Nick said. "Have you heard back from Dan?" he asked. It was the other mystery they had yet to solve.

Dulcie nodded, taking a tentative first sip of her coffee. "Just a text. He said he needed some time away. He'll be back in a couple days."

"That's not like him," Nick said.

"No, it isn't," Dulcie agreed. "I don't relish having to tell him about all of this now, either. Not sure what his reaction will be. I imagine he's going to be devastated all over again." Dulcie sat back in her chair now after having devoured the oversized blueberry muffin in record time. She sipped her coffee thoughtfully.

"Dulcie, you know I have to ask this," Nick began. "You don't think there's any connection...."

"No!" Dulcie said sharply. She looked across the table at him now, her face softening. "I'm sorry. I'm on edge. I shouldn't have reacted like that. But honestly, no, I don't think there's a connection. I mean, I can't see how there could be. They'd only just met."

"No, I don't see it either," Nick agreed. "I just need to rule people out as much as anything else. You know how it works."

"Yes, I do know," Dulcie said. "That's why you're good at your job."

At that moment there was a knock on the door. "Who could that be?" Dulcie said. "Delivery?"

She peeked out the window and saw Johnson standing on the large stone step outside. Opening the door she said, "Morning, Adam. He's right in here."

Johnson smiled at her. "Figured so. Saw his car outside." He clomped in, habitually wiped his boots off on the doormat, then jerked his head in greeting to Nick. His attention was then immediately diverted to the paper pastry bag that now very obviously held only crumbs. "Didn't get any for me?" he said plaintively to his partner.

"Didn't know you'd be joining us," Nick replied.

"Never assume," Johnson countered.

Dulcie just rolled her eyes. She'd heard their banter now countless times. "Adam, can I get you anything?"

Johnson shook his head, in spite of his obvious desire for whatever had been in the pastry bag. "Thank you, but I just had breakfast so I'm good for the next half hour or so." He patted his rounded stomach. "Thought I'd see if there were any revelations from you two, though."

They both shook their heads. Nick wondered if Dulcie would mention her brother's odd behavior, but she did not, so he kept quiet as well. He'd fill in Johnson later, as he was sure Dulcie was well aware.

Nick slid his chair back and stood up, draining the rest of his coffee. "All right, we'd best be off," he said. He turned to Dulcie. "I posted an officer at overnight watch in the museum basement, just to keep an eye on things, and I had a word with security as well. I need to check in with them and see if anyone noticed something awry last night."

"Good," she nodded, "But they were probably more focused on everything upstairs. They make sure the staff is more heavily distributed in the galleries when we have events. Everything else downstairs would have been locked up for the night, except for Francine's workrooms. I can have the staff go through security tapes from the cameras, but that'll take some time."

"Let's hold off on that for the moment," Nick said. "No need to waste their time as of yet, or cause any undue concern amongst the staff."

Dulcie had been heading toward the door but stopped now and turned to face both men. "Why do I get the feeling, though, that neither of you is convinced that this was a simple case of an allergen causing an extreme reaction? It does happen." Dulcie had added the last part as much to convince herself as the other two.

"You're right," Johnson admitted. "Just call it the detective's sixth sense. It's like in your line of work, when an art expert knows they're looking at a forgery but can't explain why. Something just seems off." He glanced over at Nick. "Do you agree?"

Nick had been lost in thought. He refocused on them now. "Agreed," he answered. "In my mind, an adult who's dealt with a potentially deadly food allergy their whole life, to the point where they carry not one but two EpiPens with them always, isn't likely to die from that allergy. In the first place, they're too cautious. Secondly, they've played out over and over in their heads what to do, exactly, if they feel any reactions. Thirdly, they even have practice pens so that they'll know the injection process." He shook his head. "No, it isn't adding up."

Johnson opened the door and stepped outside. "Meet you over at the museum," he said and continued on toward his car.

Nick turned back to Dulcie and gave her a quick kiss. "You heading over too?" he asked.

It was Saturday, but Dulcie had made it a habit of always going to the office the morning after an event, just to tie up any loose ends. "Yes, I'd planned on it already. I'll just shower and change and see you there."

Nick began to leave when Dulcie stopped him. "Wait," she said. "What should I tell Francine? She's probably been awake most of the night, waiting to hear something."

"Just tell her what we know so far. Death by anaphylactic shock caused by a food allergy. Until we know more, it was just a 'bad accident'." He stepped down onto the pavement, then turned back again. "Dulcie, remember that this is still an open investigation," he began.

"I know, I know. I can't be speculating or saying too much to anyone," she said.

"True, but that's not what I meant," he replied.

It then dawned on Dulcie what he did mean. If this wasn't an accident, if it was murder, then anyone could be a suspect. Even Francine.

Nick knew from the look spreading across Dulcie's face that she now understood. "Exactly," he said softly, then gestured toward the door. "Lock this," he added and hurried down the sidewalk.

Dulcie had locked the door as instructed. Her hands shook as she did. "Get a hold of yourself," she admonished herself aloud. She quickly showered and dressed in khakis, flats, and a loose navy silk blouse that she gave a quick French tuck to make the outfit look a bit more put-together. She pulled her still-damp hair back with a silver barrette and realized she hadn't removed the diamond studs that she'd had on the night before. "Those work," she muttered and left them in. Throwing her cell phone, sunglasses and a few other items into her tote bag, she quickly left her townhouse.

She navigated her ancient Jeep Wrangler through the city streets to Francine's hotel. Finding a parking spot, Dulcie glanced up at the tall building, as though expecting to see Francine at one of the windows. She pulled out her phone and scrolled through the contacts, finding her friend's number.

"Dulcie!" Francine answered.

"How are you?" Dulcie asked. It was useless to wish her a 'good morning' as there was very little good about it.

"I've been awake most of the night and when I did fall asleep I'd wake up thinking it was all a terrible dream, only to realize that it was real. It's just awful," Francine replied.

"Yes, it is," Dulcie said. "Listen, I'm actually out in front of your hotel right now. I don't know how you're feeling about things, but did you want to come over to the museum? Or would you rather just stay put and rest?" After Nick's warning, she tried to sound as 'normal' as possible although there was nothing normal about any of this.

Francine was silent for a moment. "I'll come with you," she finally said. "It's probably better for me to be busy," she added. "Can you give me a few minutes?"

"Sure. I'll wait down in the lobby," Dulcie replied.

"Thanks, Dulcie," Francine said as the phone clicked off.

Dulcie grabbed her bag from the car seat beside her, then went into the hotel. As she sat in a comfortable looking chair in the lobby a text lit up her phone. She purposefully kept any of the sound alerts turned off. Ostensibly it was so that she wouldn't annoy museum visitors whenever she passed through the galleries, but really it was because she couldn't stand the beeping and dinging. For her it was a source of anxiety, as though everyone was literally yelling for her attention.

She could hear Rachel's voice in her mind as she read the text. '*Am coming in today to deal with any fallout from last night. See you in a while?'* Rachel knew Dulcie would be there.

'*On my way,'* Dulcie wrote. '*Picking up Francine first.'*

Rachel gave her the thumbs-up emoji. It seemed to be her go-to response as of late. Dulcie tried to remember if she'd actually ever seen Rachel doing the real thumbs-up gesture and couldn't recall a single instance.

Dulcie tapped into her phone to Rachel, '*Could you put on coffee when you get there? Enough for Francine too?'*

Almost instantly Rachel replied, '*Already here. Doing that right now!'* She had added the coffee cup emoji. Rachel really liked her emojis it seemed.

Dulcie smiled to herself. '*Never doubted you for a second,'* she wrote.

"Dulcie!" Francine called from across the room.

Dulcie put the phone in her bag and stood, hugging her friend. "Rachel has coffee on already. We both need it, I'd say." Francine nodded her agreement as they left the hotel.

The streets of Portland were getting busy now, typical for a warm, sunny Saturday in June. Tourists had started flooding the city again as was the case each year as spring turned to summer. Dulcie parked her Jeep near the front of the museum rather than in her usual spot in the lot around back. She didn't want Francine to think about Bella's body being carried out of the loading dock the night before.

They entered through the front door and saw Rachel at the reception desk. "I'm just covering for a few minutes here," she said. "Jamal is on this morning. He's getting tea," she added.

"Can you come in and chat when he gets back?" Dulcie asked.

"Of course," Rachel said.

"Has the news spread about...," Dulcie began.

Rachel interrupted so that Dulcie wouldn't have to finish her sentence. "Haven't heard a word yet," she responded quickly, attempting to appear nonchalant. "I've only been here about twenty minutes at the most, though."

"Thanks," said Dulcie. She realized that she was about to give Rachel the thumbs-up gesture and stopped herself, jerking her hand back down into her tote bag.

Rachel's brow furrowed. "You ok?" she asked.

"Um, yeah. Just need coffee," Dulcie said and led Francine into the back hallway.

Dulcie hadn't even pulled her laptop from her bag when Rachel came striding in with two coffee mugs. Francine had sunk into the soft leather chair opposite Dulcie's desk

"That was quick," Dulcie said.

"I'm that good," Rachel quipped.

Francine gratefully took her mug and sipped from it. "I know I have a million things that I should be doing right now, but I can't think of a single one at the moment," she said.

Dulcie sat down and opened her computer. "Well, the police may have already covered this, but the first thing would be to notify next of kin, I think," Dulcie said.

"That's just it," Francine replied. "I don't think there are any. Bella talked about growing up in foster homes. If she has, or had, any relatives, she didn't know about them."

"That's so sad!" Rachel exclaimed.

"It is," Francine said. "Bella told me once that she'd grown used to moving from one home to another, but I don't see how anyone can get used to that."

"I agree," said Dulcie, "Although that may have helped her when she decided to make a move all the way across the Atlantic. Most people can't even contemplate that sort of thing. Plus, it was a good move for her - I know she really enjoyed her job as a seamstress for the Royal Opera."

"True," Francine admitted. She was glad to have at least partially contributed to Bella's happiness, if only for a short while.

Rachel snapped her fingers. "What about that couple that came to visit a few days before the opening? They were friends with Bella, right?"

Dulcie thought for a moment. "I'd forgotten all about them," she said. "The wife had gone to school with Bella and the husband was meeting with Steve, one of our board members," she added, explaining to Francine. "Rachel, can you contact him and get their information?"

"On it!" said Rachel scurrying out.

Dulcie turned to Francine. "How are the others on your crew doing?" she asked.

"As you can imagine," Francine said. "Pretty shaken up. None of them was really close to Bella outside of work, but she was always very pleasant to work with, and did her job well. Everyone liked her."

"I can see that," Dulcie replied.

Both women looked up at the sound of a tap on the doorway. Nick stood there, jacket in hand, with Johnson's large frame looming behind him. "Can we speak with you for a moment?" Nick asked.

Francine began to stand, as she said, "Of course, I should get downstairs and…"

"Actually, could we speak to both of you," Nick clarified.

"Oh!" Francine said, sitting back down.

The men entered and Nick pulled up a chair closer to Dulcie's desk. Johnson chose to stand, leaning against the door he had just closed behind them.

Nick took a deep breath. "I have to preface this by saying that there may be nothing to it, no need for concern at all, but we do need to follow up on anything that seems, well… odd."

Francine and Dulcie exchanged nervous glances.

Nick continued. "It seems that yesterday, earlier in the day, one of the opera singers came in for a costume fitting."

Francine nodded. "Yes, that was Antonio."

"Right," Nick replied. "I have to ask you, Ms. Belmont, what happens during a typical fitting?"

Francine looked startled. "I'm not sure what you mean. They change into the costume, and we mark the clothes with chalk or pins if they need to be adjusted."

"How do they usually change into the clothes?" Nick asked. He didn't suggest anything, just waited for an answer.

Francine looked at him oddly and said, "There's typically a screen in the room that they can change behind."

"Of course," Nick said. "And was there one in the workroom downstairs where Bella was?"

"Why, yes, certainly!" Francine said. "I'm not sure where you're going with this," she replied.

Dulcie wasn't sure either and wasn't happy about it. She could see that Francine was uneasy.

"I don't mean to make you uncomfortable Ms. Belmont. The reason why I ask is that one of the security guards walked by the room and told us that he saw Antonio standing nearly naked, wearing only an open shirt and underwear, which he referred to as, quote, 'very brief briefs'," Nick said.

"What?!" Dulcie and Francine exclaimed at the same time.

Nick continued. "After the guard passed he heard someone leave the room. The guard had just turned the corner in the hallway, so he looked back around and saw that it was Bella, walking quickly down the hallway in the opposite direction."

"Do you think that Antonio tried to…," Francine began. "Wouldn't Bella have said something to someone? Me, or someone else in our group?" She was bewildered.

"Yes, one would think so," Nick replied. "And I must add that the guard did not see any strange activity, just a nearly naked man standing in a room. The door was open, and it was a costume fitting. There could have been nothing to it."

"Other than it seems Bella wanted to get the hell out of there," Dulcie interjected with a concerned voice.

"Agreed," Nick said.

"But what does this have to do with Bella collapsing from a food allergy?" Francine asked.

Nick sat back in his chair, and Dulcie saw Johnson sigh deeply. "That, we don't know," Nick said. "Probably nothing. But as I mentioned, we just need to follow up on anything that seems out of place or unusual. At this point, it seems to be simply a case of unfortunate circumstances leading to Bella's death. That's probably the way this will all turn out. We just need to follow up on anything that seems out of place."

Francine looked as though she was about to cry again. Dulcie reached over and covered her friend's hand with her own.

"We supposedly emotionless Brits pride ourselves on the 'stiff upper lip' and all that," she sniffed. "I don't know what's come over me. I just felt as though I had some sort of responsibility to look after Bella once I'd heard about her background. I feel as though I've failed her."

Nick reached into this pocket and pulled out a pristine white linen handkerchief. Dulcie remembered the first time she had seen him do this – when she had been crying because a good friend of hers had died. She hadn't even really met Nick at that point, and didn't know they would become so close. But it was a kind and understanding gesture, probably the nicest thing that a near-stranger could do to help another person who was hurting. Dulcie wondered how many others Nick had helped with the same gesture. She was grateful, once again, to have him in her life.

Francine snuffled into the handkerchief. It was soft and warm. It reminded her of her grandfather who always wore linen shirts. "I'm so sorry," she said to the others.

"No need to apologize," Johnson said in what Dulcie had come to recognize as his 'kindly' voice. "It's a shock to everyone. Young people aren't supposed to die. It doesn't make sense when they do."

Francine nodded in agreement but said nothing.

Nick stood, and Johnson pushed himself away from leaning on the door, realizing that it was their cue to leave. "If either of you think of anything that seems odd or out of place with the events of last night, please let us know," Nick said. He put his card on the desk beside Francine. "You can call here or just get in touch with Dulcie," he said to her.

Again, Francine nodded but couldn't speak. Nick was nearly out the door when she swallowed hard and managed to say, "Oh, your handkerchief!" She held it out to him as he turned back.

Nick shook his head. "Yours to keep," he said. "I've got lots more." He closed the door softly behind him.

Francine snuffled her nose into the cloth once more, looking up at Dulcie through watery eyes. "He's a keeper, you know," she said.

Dulcie laughed gently. "Oh yes, I know," she replied. "It took me a little while, but believe me, now I know!"

Color is my day-long obsession, joy and torment.
To such an extent indeed that one day,
finding myself at the deathbed of a woman
who had been and still was very dear to me,
I caught myself in the act of focusing on
her temples and automatically analyzing
the succession of appropriately graded
colors which death was imposing
on her motionless face.

~ Claude Monet

CHAPTER EIGHT

"Preliminary forensic report is in," announced Johnson. His desk and Nick's faced each other in the busy police office, enabling easier communication within the sometimes noisy space. Typically police staff were coming and going through the room, talking on phones, or having extended conversations about the quality of the coffee, or lack thereof.

Nick had just eased into his desk chair and rolled forward to access his computer as Johnson spoke. He stopped midway, hands hovering over the keyboard. "And?" he queried.

"It's good," Johnson said without looking up.

Nick sighed and dropped his hands down onto the desk. "Good meaning case closed, or good meaning we've got work to do?"

Johnson wiggled his eyebrows. "Think you know the answer to that," he replied.

"All right, lay it on me," Nick said.

Johnson adjusted his reading glasses and squinted slightly at the computer screen in front of him. His ancient office chair squeaked as he leaned forward in it as much as the girth of his midsection would allow. "Cause of death was asphyxiation cause by anaphylactic shock brought on by an allergen. Swelling in the throat, mouth, face. Rash on the chest area."

"So far that sounds like what we already know, or could easily guess," Nick interrupted.

"Ah yes, but here's where it gets interesting," Johnson continued. "Stomach contents consisted of an apple and some champagne. That's it. No nuts."

"Huh," Nick muttered. "Anything else?"

Johnson scanned the rest of the report. "Some bruising on the leg…injection sites for both EpiPens located, appears they were used correctly…some bruising around the mouth…that's pretty much it for now. The usual 'more tests to follow' so we'll see what else those can tell us."

"So she died of a nut allergy with no nuts?" Nick mused.

"Well, she died of some kind of allergy. Maybe an insect bite or a sting?" Johnson said.

"Any mention of something like that on her skin?" Nick asked.

Johnson peered at the screen again, scrolling back up to the top of the report. "Nope. Only thing close is a couple of pricks on one finger, but not deep. Consistent with a sewing needle. Probably an occupational hazard," he said.

Nick remembered the costume fitting with Antonio that Bella had left abruptly. If she had been trying to work quickly in an uncomfortable situation, she could easily have poked herself with the needle. "Think a toxin could have been introduced through the needle?" he asked Johnson.

"Yeah, I was thinking the same thing, but I don't think so. It was hours later when she collapsed. Usually an allergic reaction happens pretty quickly," he replied.

"Still, we should get a toxicology report on tissue around the pricked areas," Nick said. "And have forensics check again for insect bites."

"I'll let 'em know," Johnson said, now typing with two fingers on his keyboard.

Knowing that Johnson's task would require a few extra minutes than normal given his excruciatingly slow typing, Nick got up and went across the room to the coffee maker. He picked up the half-full carafe and sniffed it to gauge how long it had been sitting there, determined that it was probably palatable, and poured two cups of coffee. He then crossed back through the office and put one down by his partner who grunted his thanks.

Johnson paused for a moment, his eyes darting across the screen while his lips moved silently as he read through the message, then he definitively hit the send button. "Done," he said, picking up the coffee cup. He took a quick swig and made a face at the bitterness. "Sent a copy to you too," he said after forcing himself to swallow.

"Thanks," Nick replied. "Let's get over to the hotel now and have a look at her room. See if we can turn up anything there that might be helpful."

"And stop for a decent coffee on the way?" Johnson asked plaintively.

"And stop for a decent coffee on the way," Nick agreed.

Johnson followed his partner out the door, but not before first quickly dumping the muddy contents of the cup into the sink beside the coffeepot and tossing the cup away.

೦೩

Rachel poked her head around the corner of the doorway to see if Dulcie was in her office.

Dulcie looked up from her desk. "Yes?" she responded.

Rachel quietly entered and sat down. Her curly hair typically bounced when she walked, but today it seemed to be lying still. She exhaled slowly.

"You all right?" Dulcie asked. "I mean, under the circumstances?"

"Yeah, all right enough, I guess," she answered. "I think it just really hit me though. It seems so wrong. Bella was young and so pretty and talented and smart, plus she had a great career ahead of her. Seems like such a waste."

"That, it does," Dulcie agreed. "Did you manage to track down that couple that visited?" she asked, changing the subject slightly. Dulcie knew that Rachel liked to stay busy, especially when dealing with difficult situations.

"Yup, just sent it to you before I came in," Rachel replied.

"Ah yes, here it is," Dulcie said, checking her email. "Jessica and Devin James. Let's just do a quick search and see if she has a website or something." Dulcie tapped on her keyboard. "Hmmmm! Interesting. Evidently she's been designing for a few years at a couple of fashion houses and is revealing her first collection next week."

"Yeah, nothing to see yet though. All very hush hush to create a buzz, I assume," Rachel said.

"Good point. Just the collection name, I see here: *Celestial*. Sounds kind of mysterious," Dulcie commented. "Some of her past work looks nice though. Nothing exciting, but I'd wear it."

Rachel burst out laughing. "Do you realize what you just said about yourself?" she exclaimed.

Dulcie started laughing too. "That's not what I meant! But maybe... ok, I admit. My wardrobe is not terribly exciting. No wait, those shoes I wore, the snakeskin ones. Those were exciting!"

Rachel nodded enthusiastically in mock agreement. "They brought down the house! Everyone was talking about them!" she declared in a breathless voice.

"Oh shut up," Dulcie replied. "Go away. I have to make a phone call."

Rachel, still snickering, left the room but then stuck her head back around again. "Seriously though, they were pretty awesome shoes. Nick must have liked them!" She grinned.

"Go!" Dulcie said pointing to the door. Rachel reached over and closed it firmly behind her, but Dulcie could hear her still giggling in the hallway.

ജ

Jessica James surveyed the wall of hastily taken photographs with a critical eye. She had to determine two things. First, the model she had selected for each look had to be the perfect one to best display it. Second, the order that they were sent down the runway had to be absolutely correct. It was a show, after all, and it needed to have an opening, a middle, and then a stunning finale.

The last part was easy. She had finished the dress the day before. It was a dark but glistening ballgown suitable for only the most elegant red-carpet occasion. Jessica was absolutely in love with it.

The problem that she was having was that the rest of the looks didn't seem to be faring as well in comparison. She kept rearranging the photos in different orders trying to make everything build and lead in to the last dress, but nothing seemed to be working.

Devin came in and stood beside her as he looked at the wall silently. "Nothing's going to even come close," he finally said. "Why don't you arrange them by color, or length or something? It would be a totally different perspective from what's usually done."

It was a good idea. Jessica was annoyed at herself for not having thought of it. She took most of the photos down, then began pinning them back up again in color groupings. The collection ranged from a few garments in a soft shell-pink to the deep blue of the closing dress. She began with the pink, transitioned to a softer blue, then a more intense blue print with elements of the pink, then finally the dark blue. She stood back. "If I accessorize right I can make the color transitions less obvious," she thought aloud.

"I think you've got it now," Devin said. "Looks great!" he said encouragingly.

Jessica heard her cell phone ring and ran across the room to her desk. It was a number that was unfamiliar. She was annoyed, unhappy with the interruption but unwilling to let anything go to voicemail so close to her scheduled show. If there were any issues, she needed to know about them as soon as possible.

"This is Jessica," she announced bluntly into the phone.

Dulcie was slightly taken aback by the abrupt salutation. "Hi Jessica, this is Dulcie Chambers from the Maine Museum of Art. I'm sure you're very busy right now, so I won't take up much of your time."

"Yes, I am," Jessica said in a clipped voice. "Can I help you with something?"

Dulcie paused for a moment. She hadn't thought ahead as to how she would phrase the conversation. "No, I just wanted to give you some sad news before you potentially ran across it second-hand. I know you were friends with one of the staff members from the Royal Opera Company, Bella Washington."

Jessica froze. "Yes, we went to design school together," she said.

Dulcie continued. "Well, I'm sorry to tell you that Bella passed away."

"Oh my god!" Jessica said. Devin looked up sharply, hearing the concern in his wife's voice. "What happened?" she asked.

"She evidently had an allergic reaction to something that brought on an anaphylactic response. She had used an EpiPen, but it wasn't enough."

"Oh, I'm so sorry to hear that!" Jessica said. "My husband sometimes has a rash when he eats shellfish so I know food allergies can be awful!"

"Yes, it can be pretty dangerous from what I understand," Dulcie said. "I'm sorry to bring you the sad news, and sorry for your loss of a friend as well."

"Thank you. We hadn't seen each other since she moved to London, but I always enjoyed her company. I know she'll be missed. I appreciate you calling," Jessica said.

"Of course," Dulcie responded. "Good luck with your new collection. I'm looking forward to seeing the photos online."

"Thanks so much. And thanks again for calling," Jessica said.

Dulcie replied in kind and Jessica hung up the phone.

"What was that about?" Devin asked.

Jessica slowly shook her head, joining him again at the wall of photos. "Bella, my friend from school that we bumped into in Maine at that museum. It seems she died."

"Really?" Devin said. "I heard you mention my shellfish allergy. Was that how she died?"

"Something like that. The museum director that we met up there just said it was an allergic reaction. That was all," she answered. She unpinned two photos and swapped them, then stood back.

"Huh, that's too bad," Devin said. "She seemed like a nice person," he added.

"Yes, she was," Jessica confirmed. She was focused on her work again.

Devin glanced out the window and realized the sun was setting. "Thoughts for dinner? You staying here or want to go out?"

Jessica glanced over at him. "You know I have too much to do right now. But I'd love it if you could scare up some sushi."

"Coming right up," Devin said and strode out of the room.

Standing alone again in the studio as the sky turned from a bright blue to a darker, softer shade, Jessica now went over to the window. She saw one star twinkling, then another emerged. '*Cellestial*,' she thought. The perfect name for her collection. '*And it will make me a star, too.*'

Don't spend time beating on a wall,
hoping to transform it into a door.

~ Coco Chanel

CHAPTER NINE

Antonio loudly gargled the ghastly concoction that he always used to clear out his throat and spit into the sink, his usual routine before working with the voice coach. He did his buzzing and humming drills as he dressed. He had just begun with the scales when he heard a knock on the door.

"Dammit," he muttered. "She's early today." It annoyed him when people did not appear at the appropriate time. His voice coach seemed to be growing more and more erratic as the days passed, to the point where he was considering finding a new one. She was good, however, and comparatively cheap, which was equally as important. Antonio still needed to watch every penny.

He pulled open the door with more force than necessary, ready to greet her with mild admonishment. Instead the words died in his mouth as he stood in front of two men.

"Sorry to bother you," the younger one said, "But are you Anthony Gallagher?"

He had used Antonio's legal name rather than his stage name. "Who is asking?" Antonio said suspiciously.

Nick pulled out his badge, as did Johnson. "Detectives Nicholas Black and Adam Johnson," Nick replied calmly. "Do you have a moment?"

Antonio hesitated, then stepped back. "Come in," he said. "What does this concern?"

"We're just following up with people who attended an event at the art museum. The event that you performed at, I believe." Both Nick and Johnson had been there, of course, but they didn't think that Antonio would have noticed them. They would have been too unimportant.

"Yes, I sang the aria from *Turandot*," he said with a hint of arrogance. He assumed neither of these men were sophisticated enough to know what he was talking about.

"*Nessun dorma*," Johnson replied, nodding. "No one sleeps," he translated. "Calaf has correctly answered Turandot's three riddles so she has to marry him unless she can find out his name by sunrise, so she keeps everyone up all night hoping someone will know." Johnson said, then smiled winningly.

Antonio looked stunned. "You know your opera," he finally admitted.

"Classic," Johnson simply stated.

Nick wasn't sure if his partner was referring to the opera itself or Antonio's assumption that he and Johnson were uneducated idiots. Perhaps both. Nick decided to quickly change the subject. "Unfortunately, Mr. Gallagher, a woman passed away sometime after your performance," Nick said. "She worked for the Royal Opera Company as the head seamstress. Perhaps you remember her?"

Of course Antonio remembered her. The seamstress that had initially annoyed him, but to whom he was unmistakably attracted, and really, who wouldn't be? That beautiful dark skin, those glowing eyes? Lips of an angel? He was quickly jerked from his vision of Bella by Nick's voice continuing on.

"I believe you met her earlier in the day for a costume fitting?" he said.

Antonio nodded. Yes, there was that.

"We were told that you had disrobed to an unusual extent," Nick said bluntly.

Antonio's sharp intake of breath was audible. "Look," he began, "I'm a performer. We see the body simply as a tool to convey a story. I resent the fact that you would imply I was untoward in any way."

"My apologies," Nick murmured. "So your only interaction with the seamstress, Bella Washington, was for the costume fitting prior to the performance?"

"Absolutely," Antonio stated, folding his arms across his chest.

"You didn't see her later in the evening, perhaps when you changed out of your costume?" Nick asked.

"Absolutely not," Antonio said. "In fact, I was talking with the baritone about the performance while I was downstairs changing back into my clothes. You can ask him. We walked back upstairs together."

Nick turned to Johnson. "Anything else we need to know?" he said.

"Nope," Johnson replied. "Not right now."

They heard a knock on the door. "That will be my voice coach," said Antonio. "If you *gentlemen*," he gave a sneering emphasis to the word, "Will excuse me, I need to get on with my work." He opened the door pointedly.

Nick and Johnson exited, leaving a bewildered looking middle-aged woman to enter after them. The door closed behind her.

"A *'tool to convey a story'*?" Nick repeated with annoyance.

"I'd say the 'tool' part is accurate," Johnson replied.

Nick snorted in response as they left the apartment building and continued out onto the street. They walked to the end of the block and rounded the corner before speaking again. Long gaps in their conversations had become a habit. It inhibited anyone from overhearing a full discussion.

"Do you believe him?" Johnson finally asked.

"I'm inclined not to," Nick replied. "He took offence pretty quickly, which usually means they're lying in some way."

"Agreed," Johnson said. "Would he have motive to kill her?" He asked. It was the first time they had strayed into a discussion of murder rather than just an accidental death.

"For some, all it takes is a bruised ego for them to snap," Nick said. "I think I could see that happening here. Bella was a beautiful young woman, certainly, and our friend Antonio seems to feel he's entitled in some way."

"Well, he is a star, after all," Johnson joked.

"How could I forget," Nick said. "I can check with that other performer to see if Antonio's story is accurate."

"It probably is," Johnson countered. "But who's to say he didn't slip back downstairs again? And he might not have intentionally harmed Bella. Could still have been the result of an unfortunate accident."

"One that he may have precipitated?" Nick asked. "You're thinking a romantic encounter on his part that she might have rebuffed?"

"Yep. And come to think of it, didn't the forensics report mention bruising around the mouth? Could have been someone trying to forcefully kiss her," Johnson said.

"Very good point," Nick nodded.

They walked along in silence for another block. Their usual coffee shop was across the street. Without even glancing at each other they both crossed and went in. Johnson slid into their usual booth while Nick went to the counter. It was a standard routine now.

Returning with two mugs, Nick put them down on the table then slid onto the bench opposite Johnson. At that moment he realized something was different. "Hey, you always sit on this side," he said. It was the bench facing toward the door.

"Yeah, thought I'd shake things up a little," Johnson mused. "Can't get too set in our ways now, can we." He sipped his coffee. "Besides, I'm trying to see this differently. We've gone from accidental death to murder pretty fast here."

"True, but don't you agree things have been adding up less and less?" Nick said.

"To the point where we're getting down toward subtraction," Johnson quipped.

"And here's the other piece I don't like," Nick added. "Dulcie's brother is still M.I.A."

Johnson's eyebrows flew up. "Huh? Missing in action?"

Nick filled him in on the backstory. "So he's not really 'missing' at this point, but he isn't here, and there isn't a good explanation yet for why he took off so fast."

"So you're thinking that if he had some sort of crazy crush on Bella, he possibly, *maybe* could have forcibly kissed her down in the basement of the museum, then some kind of unfortunate accident involving a nut allergy occurred and he took off?" Johnson looked at Nick incredulously.

"I know, I know. Seems totally out of character. But while he isn't here, he has to at least be a 'person of interest' until we can rule him out," Nick said.

"Dulcie won't like that," Johnson said quietly.

"She already doesn't," Nick admitted. "I mentioned that Dan's behavior was odd, as well as coincidental to Bella's death."

Johnson's eyes widened. "How'd she take that?" he asked.

"Relatively ok. She knows how this process works. I didn't mention anything about foul play though, just that we needed to talk with him as soon as possible to get all the facts. She understands that," Nick said.

"Don't envy you though," Johnson muttered. "Rock and a hard place," he added.

"Don't I know it," Nick sighed.

ॐ

"Did you get in touch with the couple in New York?" Rachel asked. She sat on the soft leather chair by Dulcie's desk.

"I did," Dulcie said.

"How'd it go?" Rachel asked.

Dulcie thought for a moment. "Kind of strange, actually, although I'm not well versed in telling someone that their friend has died, so I have very little to go on for comparison."

"I'm glad to hear that part!" Rachel said. "How was it strange? Was she upset?"

"Yes and no. She definitely sounded surprised, but I'm not sure I would say she was upset. Although, she did seem distracted. She's probably putting the final touches on her new collection, so I'm sure she's very focused on that," Dulcie said. "Maybe the news I gave her hadn't really sunk in while we were still talking."

"When we're about to open a new exhibit, I can barely get your attention," Rachel responded. "I'd say she's a workaholic like you are."

Dulcie's eyes widened. "What? I'm a workaholic?"

Rachel nodded her head several times so quickly that her curly hair bounced up and down erratically.

"Well it takes one to know one," Dulcie muttered.

"Thank you, I consider that a compliment!" Rachel stated firmly. "It all seems weird though. I mean, Bella died but everything else continues on. I feel like we should be doing something else for her."

Dulcie swiveled her office chair back and forth. "I agree," she said.

Francine appeared in the doorway. "I couldn't help but overhear those last few words," she said. "Sorry, not eavesdropping, just a quiet walker," she added.

"No, that's fine," Dulcie said. "Maybe you can help. You knew Bella much better than we did. I spoke with that friend of hers from New York who had just reconnected with her here in the museum. Is there anyone else she was close with? Maybe in London, or back at her old design school in New York?"

"Not really," Francine replied thoughtfully. "She kept to herself for the most part. Always very pleasant, but quiet." She paused, then said, "She did mention several times a professor in New York. I think his guidance had an impact on her, and I remember it because that's how you and I met, Dulcie, in one of my classes."

"I loved your class!" Dulce exclaimed. "Do you know if Bella continued to be in touch with him?"

"Perhaps, off and on. I remember his name was Gerald Feldman. He was one of Bella's references, and I contacted him when I was considering hiring Bella. We had quite a good conversation, as I recall. Very pleasant, knowledgeable man."

Dulcie glanced at Rachel who had already risen from her chair. She simply nodded at Dulcie and left.

Francine watched her abrupt departure. "Oh goodness! Did I say something wrong?" she asked.

Dulcie laughed. "Not at all. Rachel is now looking up Mr. Feldman's information which she'll send to me in a matter of minutes," she replied.

Francine sat in the chair that Rachel had just vacated. "You've found the perfect assistant, then. As I thought I had," she trailed off.

"Rachel is a gem, that's for sure," Dulcie said. "I'm sure that you and Bella were getting to that point as well."

"I think we were," Francine replied. "But there was always something reserved about her. She never quite opened up. She was very smart, very talented, very cordial and polite with everyone, but I never felt as though she would let anyone be a friend."

Dulcie was concerned that Francine would begin crying again, but the woman just shook her head softly as though to gently clear away the thoughts. She put both hands on the arms of the chair and pushed herself up. "Best get on with things," she said. "Do let me know if you're able to contact Mr. Feldman. I think he goes by 'Gerry' if I remember correctly?"

Dulcie looked at her friend with concern, but then realized that, like herself, Francine got through the difficult times in life by throwing herself into her work. It was probably all part of being a 'workaholic' as Rachel would undoubtedly remind her. Dulcie smiled at her friend. "Thank you," she replied. "I'll let you know what he says."

Ȕȓ

Dan Chambers steered the yacht slowly back into Portland harbor. He'd lost track of time but realized now as he watched a commuter ferry leave the terminal that it was Monday. He'd been aimlessly motoring around Casco Bay all weekend, anchoring only a few times in small coves to eat or sleep.

Not that he'd eaten much. He'd been hit hard by his feelings toward Bella. He thought that they'd been hitting it off when he first met her and talked with her while taking Dulcie's group out on the boat. That she'd refused him so bluntly afterwards was a surprise. Then, to see her again at the museum event so soon after, and in the arms of someone else… it had been a gut punch.

He'd needed time to let his thoughts settle. He didn't understand why it had made such an effect on him. There had been many women in his life, but they'd all been the same type: pretty, fun-loving, and temporary.

Maybe he just wasn't cut out for a life with someone else. Maybe some people were destined to be alone, essentially, all their lives. Maybe he'd screwed everything up and wasted too much time. Maybe it was too late.

Dan realized he was approaching his wharf and turned the wheel sharply. The bow came around and he eased into the slip. Throwing the motor into neutral, he jumped down the steps from the bridge to the deck, quickly grabbed the bow line and tossed it around the cleat on the dock. Tying it off, he dropped the bumpers over the side between the hull and the dock, then caught the stern line on another cleat. He went back up to the bridge and shut the motor off.

From her office window, Dulcie watched Dan's maneuvering. He was a natural on the water. He always had been.

She wondered if she should open the window and call out to him, or if she should just wait for him to get in touch with her. She decided on the latter – if he'd needed time and space, she shouldn't rush him. She knew her brother all too well. He'd get in touch when he was ready. Dulcie was just relieved to see him back.

The sun is up, the sky is blue.
It's beautiful, and so are you.

~ John Lennon

CHAPTER TEN

Nick pulled the boxes of Chinese food from the paper bag and put them on the table. Dulcie watched as he opened them one by one, peering inside each time and saying, "Nope."

"You know it'll be the last one you open," Dulcie said. She poured a glass of wine for him, then filled her own glass. She'd chosen a sauvignon blanc that she'd chilled to an extra-cold temperature in the freezer. She knew it was a favorite of Nick's.

"Got it!" Nick exclaimed.

"Finally!" Dulcie said. "Now which is the chicken fried rice?"

"Ummmm," Nick replied with a bewildered look as he scanned the table.

"Never mind!" Dulcie laughed. She also peered into the containers until she located it.

They ate straight from the boxes. They'd ordered Chinese often enough to know that they liked completely different things, which made it easy. Dulcie unwrapped her wooden chopsticks and dove into her rice.

"So here's my news," she said in between bites. "Dan's back."

"Really?" Nick paused for a moment, glancing up at her over his pad thai. "When? Have you talked with him?"

Dulcie shook her head, swallowing. "I saw him come in and dock the boat around midday. I didn't try to get in touch or yell down or anything, though. Figured I'd wait for him to be ready to talk."

"Probably a good idea," Nick agreed. He took a sip of wine. "I love this!" he exclaimed. "It's that New Zealand one, right?"

Dulcie nodded, her mouth full.

Nick's phone buzzed. He put down the wine glass and pulled it out of his shirt pocket. "Speak of the devil. It's your brother," he said. "Hi Dan," he answered into the phone.

Dulcie could hear her brother's voice but couldn't make out what he was saying.

"Yeah, I'm over at Dulcie's," Nick replied into the phone. "Sure, c'mon over." He glanced up at Dulcie who nodded vigorously. "See you in a few," Nick added and put the phone back in his pocket.

Dulcie knew that the walk to the museum, and therefore the dock beside it where Dan kept the yacht, took exactly twelve minutes. She enjoyed walking to work through the city streets on nice days, and endured the commute on the blustery, wintery days when she knew that it was useless to attempt to start her beloved but ancient Jeep. Dan's legs were longer though, so he'd probably make it in under ten.

As if on cue, they heard a quick knock on the door several minutes later. Dan opened it before Dulcie could even stand up from the table.

"Hi," he said quickly, looking at the table. His stomach growled and he realized then that he had eaten very little over the past few days.

"Dan!" Dulcie exclaimed. "You had me so worried!" she was about to admonish him but Nick intervened.

"Help yourself," he said, waving his arm across the food cartons. "There's plenty, as always. We tend to over-order. Want some wine?"

"I'd love a beer if you have any?" he asked Dulcie.

"Take whatever you can find in the fridge," she said, motioning toward the kitchen.

When they heard him rummaging through the refrigerator, Nick whispered to Dulcie, "Go easy on him!"

Dulcie put down her rice container and took a sip of wine. Nick was right. Dulcie had no idea what had been going through her brother's mind, but he'd clearly been upset. She reminded herself that he had contacted her to reassure her that he was all right, but just needed some space. No, this wasn't about her worries, certainly.

When Dan returned, beer bottle in hand, she said, "I'm just glad you're back, safe and sound. Anything you want to talk about?"

Dan took a big swig from the bottle and put it down on the table. "Well first of all, I'm sorry to take off like that. But secondly, is Bella still around?"

Nick and Dulcie both froze, staring at each other. Dan didn't know. He'd left before they'd discovered Bella lying amongst the bolts of fabric in the basement of the museum. Dulcie felt the rice she'd just eaten churn now in the pit of her stomach.

Dan took one look at both of them and said, "Ok, what's up?"

"Dan," Dulcie began, "We have some bad news."

Dan laughed nervously. "Don't tell me she's run off with someone else, although given what I saw, that wouldn't surprise me."

"What you saw?" Nick asked quickly.

"Yeah, during the party, after the singers were performing. I saw her go downstairs. I wanted to talk to her one more time, so a couple minutes later, I followed her down. There was a light on in one of the rooms where the costume racks were, so I assumed she was in there. I looked in from the hallway and saw her kissing the guy who'd been singing."

"Which singer?" Dulcie asked.

"The last one. Not the one that sang the funny Figaro song. The one after that."

Nick looked intently at Dan. "Was she kissing him, or was he kissing her?"

Dan was taken aback. "Strange question!" he replied. "I didn't hang around long enough to notice. Or care, for that matter. I just took off." He picked up his bottle of beer again, taking another swig.

"Look," he continued. "I know it's stupid, especially given my background with dating, but I fell for her. Hard. It was a shock. Then I started thinking about all the women I might have hurt with my own behavior. I mean, I never led anyone on, but at the same time, I know a few were hurt when I ended relationships." He gazed down into the narrow opening of the beer bottle, watching the bubbles slowly float to the top. "I feel like she could be my redemption in a way."

'*Damn!*' thought Dulcie. '*This will crush him.*' Aloud she said, "Dan, we need to tell you something." She stopped for a moment, then continued quickly. "We found Bella unconscious that evening. She had an allergic reaction to something that caused anaphylactic shock. I'm so sorry to tell you this, but she died."

The color drained from Dan's face. He stood forcefully, knocking the chair over behind him as he did. He quickly walked across the room, wrenched open the door and went outside onto the step. He felt like he couldn't breathe.

Nick and Dulcie were behind him in an instant.

"*Jesus*," Dan muttered. "That can't be true," he said. He kept shaking his head.

Nick watched him intently. He had witnessed quite a few people being told about a death and had learned to recognize the clues of who was clearly reacting to the knowledge for the first time, and who was faking because they already knew. This was, without question, the first that Dan had known of Bella's death.

Dan sat down heavily on the cold stone step. Dulcie went back into the house, grabbed his beer, and brought it back out to him. "It'll settle your stomach" she said.

Dan drained the bottle then looked back up at them. "I can't…I mean…," he couldn't think straight.

Nick said, "We didn't know that someone else was downstairs in the basement with her before she died. Is there anything else you can remember about what you saw?"

Dan sat silent for a moment, looking bewildered. He shook his head. "No, not really," he finally replied.

The color had returned to his face now, and he stood, albeit on still wobbly legs. "I need to walk, and maybe lie down," he said. "I'm going back to the boat," he added.

Dulcie looked concerned. "Can I check on you later?" she asked.

Dan was already out on the sidewalk. "I'll text you when I'm awake again," he said. He suddenly felt exhausted.

"Promise me you will, even if it's the middle of the night!" Dulcie called after him.

Dan nodded and gave them a half wave without looking back.

Nick and Dulcie returned inside. Dulcie had lost her appetite and began clearing away her food containers. Nick did the same, then refilled their wine glasses. They moved to the living room and settled in on the couch.

"That was pretty awful," Dulcie said, fighting back tears.

Nick took her hand and held it, toying with her fingers. "Yeah, it was," he agreed.

"You've seen that before too, right? The reaction to death?" Dulcie asked.

"Variations of it, yes. A number of times." It was the worst part of his job.

Dulcie thought for a moment. "The strange part is, he barely knew Bella. Yet he'd fallen for her so hard and so fast, it seems. Is that even possible?"

Nick took a deep breath. Was it possible? Oh yes, he knew for a fact that it was certainly possible. "It's how I felt when I first saw you," he said quietly.

Dulcie had been sitting close to him, comforted by his strong, warm body leaning against hers. She pulled away slightly, enough to look up at his face. "What?" she responded with surprise.

He nodded. "It was the opening of the Winslow Homer exhibit. I saw you on the other side of the gallery. I had never believed in 'love at first sight' until then. You looked beautiful but it wasn't really about the way you looked. I felt like you were the person that I was supposed to meet, to be with. You were the other half of me."

"But you hadn't even met me yet!" Dulcie exclaimed.

"I know," Nick said. "It's kind of insane, but there it is. Kismet. Fate. Call it what you like."

"I call it amazing luck on my part!" Dulcie replied.

"I know we had a difficult start," Nick continued, "And that was my fault. But I'm glad you gave me another chance. I just didn't want to lose you."

Dulcie leaned over and kissed him softly. "You have me now, like it or not!" she said.

"Oh, I like it," Nick replied, kissing her back. "I like it very much!"

At four in the morning, Dulcie was awakened by her phone as it lit up and buzzed on her nightstand. She reached over for it and saw it was a text message from her brother:

Just woke up, doing ok. Still can't believe it. Tell Nick I remembered something. I thought I heard the man laugh after I turned away. A nasty laugh, not a nice one. He didn't see me, so I wasn't what he was laughing at.

Nick was snoring softly beside Dulcie. She wondered if she should wake him, but knew if she didn't, he might be gone before she woke up again. She nudged him gently. His eyes opened. She held the phone in front of him so he could see the message.

He read through it twice, then rubbed his eyes. "Can you send that to me?" he said quietly.

Dulcie nodded and tapped the screen. "Done," she said.

"Thanks," he replied. He gave her a quick kiss then got up. "Go back to sleep," he said. "I'll catch up with you later!"

Dulcie smiled at him. She closed her eyes, slid over to where he'd been lying, and snuggled back into the warm sheets.

*Blue is the only color which maintains
its own character in all its tones...
it will always stay blue; whereas yellow
is blackened in its shades, and fades away
when lightened; red when darkened becomes
brown, and diluted with white is no longer
red, but another color – pink.*

~ Raoul Dufy

CHAPTER ELEVEN

Nick had already been at his desk for three hours before Johnson arrived at his usual time in the morning.

"You're quite the early bird," he said to his partner, tapping his keyboard to make the computer screen spring to life.

"Yeah, up at the crack of dawn, or before actually. Got some news," he said.

"Excellent," Johnson replied. "Give me one minute to get some swill," he said, jerking his head over in the direction of the coffee pot. "Need one too?"

"No, sir. But thanks," Nick said. "I've had way too much this morning already."

Johnson lumbered across the room then came back blowing over the top of a steaming cup. "Ok, whaddya got?" He sank into his decrepit office chair and tentatively sipped the coffee.

Nick considered for a moment which piece of news to tell his partner first, the bit about Antonio or that Dan had returned. "Dulcie's brother is back," he finally said. "We saw him last night. He didn't know that Bella had died. Hit him pretty hard."

Johnson nodded in response, grimacing at the coffee.

"Dan said that he'd seen Bella kissing a man in the basement of the museum. It was that younger opera singer," Nick added.

Johnson put down the coffee cup. "The irritating one?" Johnson asked rhetorically. "Now that is news!" he said.

"Yep," Nick agreed. "That's not all, though. The toxicology report came in. Bella had antibodies in her bloodstream indicating an allergic reaction to nuts of some kind. So I checked the catering menu from that night, and they had a bread that had sesame seeds on it."

Johnson looked confused. "Sesame seeds?" he said.

"Evidently people who have nut allergies can also be allergic to other kinds of seeds and legumes. I can give you a whole rundown of what they are if you want," Nick said.

"Please don't," his partner replied. "So you think she ate some of the bread with sesame seeds?"

"No I don't," Nick answered. "First of all, it wasn't in her stomach contents. Plus, she'd have known all the potential risky foods and wouldn't have taken a chance with unknown items. Someone with a life-long food allergy knows what could kill them."

Now it dawned on Johnson what his partner was getting at. "You think our friend Antonio ate the sesame seeds, then kissed her. Huh! Is that even possible? I mean, would it be enough to kill her?"

"It could, if it was recent enough that he'd eaten it and if her allergy was severe enough," Nick said. "Evidently the allergen can remain in a person's saliva for a while."

"Well, I'll be!" Johnson said. "That's a first. Literally the kiss of death."

"Looks like it," Nick agreed.

"Question now is, did he know that, and if so, was it intentional?" Johnson asked.

"Both good questions," Nick admitted. "I thought I'd remembered seeing a medical alert bracelet on her arm when we first found her. I just checked the photos and I was right – she was wearing one. Not everyone knows what those are, though. But even if Antonio did recognize it, he wouldn't have known what it was for specifically unless he had seen it very closely."

"Or if he'd talked to her about it," Johnson thought aloud. "But that seems pretty unlikely."

"Agreed. Also, would Antonio even know that sesame seeds were a potential threat, and that he could poison her by kissing her?" Johnson mused. "I mean, we're just learning that key fact, and we're supposed to be the experts, so how could he have known, especially to the point of using it to kill her? And furthermore," Johnson paused for effect, pointing at his partner, "If Antonio didn't know that, could it even be considered murder or are we right back to where we started: accidental death?"

"Wow, that's a lot to think about. You must be exhausted!" Nick joked with his partner. Johnson wadded up a piece of paper and threw it at Nick.

Refocusing, Nick said, "It could be considered assault, maybe." His years of study at Harvard law school were now churning through his mind as he tried to remember how the process worked to bring charges on that count. Then he realized he'd forgotten to tell Johnson the final bit of information that Dan had texted. "One last thing, too. Dan remembered that after he'd seen the two of them together, he heard Antonio laughing in a nasty way," Nick added.

"Laughing at Dan?" Johnson asked.

"No, Dan doesn't think that either of them saw him," Nick replied. "He must have been laughing at something he said or did to Bella."

"That guy is a piece of work for sure," Johnson muttered.

"Yeah," Nick agreed. "Maybe we need to have another chat with him?"

"I'd be happy to take that one on," Johnson said. He'd put more than one man in his place who felt it was his male privilege to take advantage of any woman he pleased. He knew the type all too well: the bully who Johnson could easily crack with threats of jail time for the creep's actions. Johnson also had no problem carrying out those threats, seeing the fear in their eyes when they realized they were actually going to be locked up for behavior they had barely begun to realize was criminal.

"Although maybe the element of surprise with that creep would be better?" Nick considered. "Let's save it for now." He pushed himself back from his desk and stood. "I'm going back down to the museum and check out the room where we found Bella again. Maybe there's something we overlooked."

"Give my best to Dulcie," Johnson grinned.

Nick ignored him as he grabbed his phone from his desk and headed for the door.

On his walk over, Nick saw Dan's yacht tied up to the dock. '*Wonder if he's awake yet?*' he thought. He turned and went down the dock, reaching the boat just as Dan emerged from below deck.

"Ahoy," Nick said.

"Top o'the mornin'," Dan replied somewhat wearily.

Nick was glad to see Dan's characteristic sense of humor returning, even if only a little. "I saw the text you sent Dulcie. Anything else you remember?" Nick asked.

Dan motioned for Nick to join him. They both sat on the deck cushions, now warm from the morning sun shining on them. "Not really. At first I didn't want to remember any of it, but I've been forcing myself to."

"Yeah, it isn't easy," Nick agreed. "Do you think that Antonio, the singer, forced himself on Bella? I mean, did it seem like she was a willing participant?" He was trying to make it sound as clinical as possible.

"That's kind of the part that bothered me," Dan replied. "When I talked to Bella a few days ago, and then when I asked her out to dinner, she made it pretty clear that she wasn't interested. And not just that she wasn't interested in me, she wasn't interested in anyone. I actually wondered if she wasn't attracted to men, but she didn't say she was a lesbian or anything like that. It seemed more like she was a loner and just didn't want other people in her life. I think that's why I got upset when I saw her with that guy."

"It sounds like he probably did force himself on her then," Nick said. He was thinking about the forensics report and the bruising around Bella's mouth.

Dan looked out across the horizon as a seagull swooped by. "You thought it could have been me," he said quietly.

Nick knew what he meant. Dan saw it as a lack of trust, a blow to their newly formed friendship.

Nick didn't want to offer platitudes or reassurances. He respected Dan too much for that. "I had to rule you out as someone possibly involved," he said. "When you left suddenly, and we didn't have as many facts on the case, no one knew what to think. But remember that I'm trained to *not* place the blame on anyone until I have the facts. So no, I did not think it could have been you, but I did need to find the evidence to rule you out definitively."

Dan looked relieved. "Thanks. I get it. That's how your job works," he said.

Nick nodded. "That's how my job works. It isn't fun, most of the time."

"Then why do you do it?" Dan asked.

"Really good question," Nick replied. "I'm not sure. It's like solving a giant puzzle every time. And I suppose there's an element of an adrenaline rush to it as well. I also feel like I'm helping people in some way, bringing the bad guys to justice."

"As long as you don't put me in the 'bad guys' category," Dan said, "I'm ok with that."

"I doubt I'd ever be able to put you in that category. Besides, I'm a friend of the family," Nick said.

Dan grinned now. "A bit more than a friend, I'd say." He glanced up at the window of Dulcie's office.

Nick couldn't help but grin as well.

Several moments later, Nick found himself in Dulcie's office sitting in the chair by her desk. "Good morning, again," she said slyly. "What were you two talking about down there? I saw you out on the deck grinning like two Cheshire cats."

"You, of course," Nick answered.

"Stop it!" Dulcie replied. She wasn't sure whether or not to believe him. She changed the subject. "So is Dan off the hook?"

"I'd say so, yes," Nick said. "I've just informed him of that, much to his relief I'd say."

"Mine, too," Dulcie added.

"Anything of interest you've discovered?" Nick asked.

"Not really. I've been emailing with a former professor of Bella's. He was upset to hear about her. He's been reminiscing a bit. He even found some designs that she did and sent them to me. Looks like she was very talented." Dulcie tapped on her computer and brought up the images. She spun the laptop around for Nick to see.

"Wow, those are nice," Nick agreed. "Wonder why she just became a seamstress then?"

"I asked Gerry that. He's the professor, retired now. Gerald Feldman. He said that Bella never liked the competitive aspect of the fashion industry. She was a talented seamstress from the start, though, so he encouraged her there." Dulcie explained.

"Makes sense," Nick said. "All right. Mind if I go look around the room downstairs one more time? Might have missed something before."

"Sure," Dulcie replied. "Francine wants to get back in when she can. There are still a couple of costumes that didn't make it into the exhibit yet. They ran out of time before the opening so we decided to add them this week."

"Understood," Nick said. "I'll give the space one more look, then I think we can take the scary *'police line - do not cross'* tape down."

"Thank you. That'd be great," Dulcie said. "The staff is on edge enough right now as it is. Me included."

"I don't think you have anything to worry about at this point," Nick said. "We don't have any motive at all for murder."

"That's a relief!" Dulcie declared. "So it was just an awful accident?"

"Kind of, yes," Nick said.

Dulcie gave him a sideways glance. "What do you mean by '*kind of*?'" she asked. "What are you not telling me?"

Nick explained what they had discovered about Antonio, how he must have kissed Bella after having the sesame seed bread from the caterers. It wasn't intentional or premeditated, so it couldn't be classified as murder, but it could be classified as some form of assault if it had been unwanted by Bella.

"Really, kissing someone with a nut allergy after having nuts is enough to kill them?" Dulcie was a bit incredulous.

"Evidently, for some people," Nick said. "Hard for me to believe, too."

"I knew that guy was a jerk," she added. "Fabulous singer, but a creep, nonetheless. How did he respond to all of this?"

"We haven't confronted him yet," Nick said. "Still need to pin down a few more details."

"It's all kind of bizarre, not unlike an opera. How ironic."

Nick agreed. It was all too ironic. Perhaps bordering on farcical.

ᘓ

Adam Johnson's lips moved, as they always did, while he read. He never uttered anything aloud, but somehow the act of moving his mouth seemed to help him take in the words more clearly. He'd done it since childhood, a habit that many teachers had tried to coax out of him, without success. He was completely unaware of it at this point, nor did he care.

He squinted at the screen, reading the email again. It was a brief update to the toxicology report. Most of it was uninteresting. One item puzzled him, however. The level of adrenaline in Bella's body was only slightly elevated. That didn't seem right. It wasn't consistent with her having used not just one but two EpiPens.

Johnson knew that the "Epi" was short for 'epinephrine' which was the same thing as adrenaline. Historically they'd been identified and named at roughly the same time by different scientists, but one used the Latin terminology while the other used the Greek. The gland that the chemical came from in humans was above the kidney, so epinephrine was actually Greek for "above the kidney" while adrenaline was Latin, also for "above the kidney." It seemed a bit ridiculous to him that science terminology couldn't seem to get together on this one, but old habits die hard.

Be that as it may, whether it was epinephrine or adrenaline, Bella didn't have nearly enough in her system to counter the effects of the allergens. Nor did she have enough to support the fact that she used two EpiPens. Had she used one, or both, incorrectly?

Johnson took off his reading glasses just as Nick came into the police station office. "What's up?" Nick said after taking one look at his partner. Nick sat down at his desk opposite Johnson.

"A little perplexing issue is all," Johnson said. He told Nick what he'd just discovered.

"That is strange," Nick said. "We bagged the EpiPens, right?"

"Yeah. Forensics has them now," Johnson replied.

"Let's have a look at them," Nick suggested. "Let me check the forensics report right now too, in case there was something we missed about the injections."

Nick began reading through the forensics report while Johnson contacted the team. When Nick finished he said, "Nope. Looks fine. Says both injection sites were found, penetration into the skin was consistent with how the pens should work."

Johnson looked down at his screen. He'd just received an email back. "Forensics wants us to come down. They say they have something to show us," he said.

Both Nick and Johnson went through the heavy door at the back of the office and down the echoing stairwell to the bottom level of the building. Since the station sat on a hill, the lower level was partly the basement, but partly accessible to a parking lot behind the building. This meant that vehicles could drive up to the building and unload whatever was necessary without anything being visible to someone who happened by.

Johnson opened the door to a large lab area. A staff person wearing a white coat over her clothes was standing behind a counter that contained various medical instruments. She looked up from a microscope and greeted them.

"Thanks for coming down," she said. "Here's what we've got." She handed them a clear plastic bag with two EpiPens inside. "These are the pens that the deceased used. Looks like she used them correctly and they functioned fine, but here's the strange part. Check the expiration dates."

Johnson patted his shirt pocket and realized he didn't have his reading glasses. He handed the bag to Nick who looked closely at the pens. "Huh," he said. "Over five years ago. How long are these things supposed to last?" he asked.

"Not that long!" the woman said. "One study said four years at best. I know I wouldn't take the chance keeping an old one around though. Few would."

"Could someone forget that they hadn't replaced them?" Johnson wondered.

The woman shrugged. "It could happen of course, but again, the people who carry these around know that it can be a matter of life or death. When they need them, they have to work quickly and fully. Old ones can still administer a dose of adrenaline, but it might not be the full dose that the person needs. And in this case, looks like it wasn't."

"Can I just confirm that the deceased was wearing a medical alert bracelet that noted she had a severe nut allergy?" Nick asked.

"Yes, she did," the woman said. "I saw it myself. Looks like she'd had it for quite a long time – it was pretty worn. Probably never took it off."

The two detectives thanked her and went back upstairs. Sitting at their desks facing each other again, they both drummed their fingers on the desktops. "Yeah, I couldn't agree more," Nick finally said.

"With…," Johnson prompted.

"With exactly what you're thinking," Nick replied. "How is it that Bella was concerned enough to wear a bracelet all the time, likely for most of her life, but didn't replace her EpiPens in five years?"

"Not adding up," Johnson said.

"Still," Nick agreed.

*A sky as pure as water
bathed the stars and
brought them out.*

~ Antoine de Saint-Exupéry

CHAPTER TWELVE

Dulcie had been too distracted to really look at the completed exhibit. First, there was the opening party, then her brother's sudden disappearance, Bella's death, and the investigation that followed. Now, with the police tape gone and Francine's crew back in the basement rooms, they had finally put the last few costumes on the remaining mannequins and installed them upstairs in the gallery.

With renewed focus, Dulcie walked past the ornate lettering stenciled in gold on the freshly painted oyster-gray wall of the exhibit entrance. *The Costumes of Covent Garden*, it read.

She wandered amongst the mannequins, looking at the lavish garments. She had read all of the cards explaining each item before they'd been installed, but now she saw everything with fresh eyes. It amazed her that such care and painstaking work went into costumes that would only be seen up close by just a few people. Why bother with all the detail? She hadn't thought to ask the question before.

"What do you think?" Francine had sidled up beside Dulcie. She glanced over at her, then back at a scarlet red gown with elbow-length sleeves that had ruffles cascading down in layers until they nearly reached the floor.

"The exhibit is wonderful!" Dulcie said. "The work is exquisite, too."

"Bella did this one," Francine said. "She and I worked on the design together for that performance. She was an incredible seamstress and a talented designer."

"You must miss her already," Dulcie said.

"I do," Francine agreed. "She understood how crucial a costume is. So many people enter costume design thinking that it's all for the audience, but it isn't. The costume is critical to the performer. They use it to create their character, to really become their character. Imagine trying to play The Wicked Witch of the West while wearing Cinderella's ballgown."

Dulcie laughed, thinking what that would look like.

"That's why costume designers put in the level of detail you see. That part is for the performers, not the audience," Francine continued. "You should see what happens when they try on their costumes for the first time before a new show. You can literally watch their personalities change as they just slide into character. It can be a little disconcerting!"

"I suppose we all do that in a way," Dulcie said. "We get dressed up to go to an event, then behave a certain way according to what we're wearing, whether it's a cocktail party or a baseball game."

"Exactly," Francine agreed. "Although I've never been to a baseball game!" she laughed. "I supposed it's not unlike the kit you see at a cricket match."

"Yes, it is," Dulcie confirmed. "Right down to the face-painting."

"There you are!" Rachel's voice carried through the gallery in a loud whisper. Several visitors turned to look at her and Dulcie put a finger to her lips. She didn't like to interrupt other peoples' experience of the exhibits.

"Sorry!" Rachel mouthed almost silently. Francine and Dulcie followed her back into the cavernous foyer of the museum. "Just wanted to let you know that Bella's friend, the designer we met, has her show this afternoon. It's going to be live-streamed on her website, in case you want to see."

"Sounds interesting," Francine said. "I'd love to see it."

"Three o'clock," Rachel informed them.

"Let's watch in my office," Dulcie said. "We'll have a little viewing party."

"Nice!" Rachel nearly squealed. "I'll get a big screen from tech that we can hook up so we don't have to crowd around your tiny laptop." She hurried off.

"I'm going to begin the laborious process of cleaning up the workspace downstairs," Francine said. "I'll be back up later."

Dulcie went back into the gallery and continued to wander. She was lost in thought when she heard Nick's voice behind her. "This was the room, and you were standing in that very spot," he said in a hushed voice.

She turned around and smiled at him but looked confused. "Sorry, what are you…?" She then realized what he meant.

"When I fell in love with you," he said. "Before I'd even met you."

Dulcie realized that neither of them had used the "L" word before. It had been implied, increasingly, as it was now, but neither had said the actual word to the other.

"And do you now?" she asked.

"Do I what?" he replied. He was daring her to say it. He held his breath.

"Do you love me?" she finally asked.

"Do you love me?" he replied.

"I asked first," she quipped.

"I already said so," he answered.

Dulcie couldn't stop the grin that spread across her face. "Yes, Nick. It took me a little while to realize it, but yes, I do love you!"

"Well then, I love you too," he said. He reached down and held both of her hands He wanted to kiss her, badly. He glanced around to see if they were alone. They were not. Museum visitors were wandering around the gallery.

Nick growled. "*Dammit*," he swore softly.

Dulcie giggled. She felt as though she was floating.

"Did you come here just to tell me that?" she said.

He laughed and let go of one of her hands. "No, but I've been wanting to say it for a long time."

"Me too," Dulcie said. "But we can always continue this conversation later," she winked at him.

"I'd be very happy to," he replied. "In the meantime, let me fill you in on something new with the case." They were now wandering back to Dulcie's office. "It seems that Bella used EpiPens that were quite old, which could explain why they didn't save her."

"How old is 'quite old'?" Dulcie asked.

"About five years," Nick answered.

"Wow. I know nothing about them, but that does seem old. Weird, because Francine was just talking to me about Bella's attention to detail," Dulcie said.

"Maybe that only applied to her work?" Nick suggested.

"Possibly, but it seems strange," Dulcie replied. "Perfectionism usually applies across the board."

They both turned as Rachel came noisily into Dulcie's office carrying a large video screen. The cord dragged along the floor behind her. She plunked it down at one end of Dulcie's desk. "Hi Nick! We're gonna watch a fashion show. Wanna join?" She began untangling the cords on the back, not waiting for an answer.

"Bella's friend Jessica, the one from New York, is showing her collection today. It will be live-streamed on her website. We thought it would be fun to watch," Dulcie explained.

"As much as I would enjoy that, I'm afraid I have to get going," Nick said with mock sincerity.

Rachel rolled her eyes.

"All right, I'll speak with you later," Dulcie told him. Thanks for the update, and the, um…uh, revelation!" she added.

Nick tried to stop the broad smile spreading across his face but couldn't. He could feel his cheeks turning red as well. He was very glad that Rachel was now hidden behind the screen.

At three o'clock, Dulcie, Rachel, and Francine all sat comfortably in Dulcie's office. Rachel had linked her laptop to the large screen and now brought up the website of Jessica James.

A stylized JJ intertwined with lots of curly whisps appeared on the screen. The letters began to move around each other and grow, as though they were vines, then the image faded to show a title that read: Click here to see the collection! Rachel clicked on it, and a video window popped up. The audience had just assembled and they watched the lights dim. The same JJ that they'd seen on the opening page of the website had been stenciled on the scrim at the end of the runway.

Upbeat but romantic music began, setting the mood of the show. The first model strutted out. Dulcie thought that her shell-pink dress with soft blue accessories was pretty, but didn't seem very groundbreaking. The second look was a lovely silk shirtdress, this time in a blue pattern with pink accents. Dulcie glanced at Rachel and Francine. Neither of them seemed very impressed either.

They watched the next few models pace down the runway, twirling at the end. Then, the music changed to something more mysterious and the color palette changed as well. The colors were darker now, all blue but increasingly deeper shades with each new look. The designs were more detailed as well, less flowy and simplistic.

When the finale dress appeared on the screen, all three women watching gasped. It was exquisite. A gorgeous gown of an intensely beautiful blue shade, it had tiny crystal beads sewn to it strategically so that it sparkled in the light. A ruffle, also glittering with beads, cascaded from one shoulder, around the model, and descended effortlessly to the floor. "Stunning!" Francine said.

The models all walked out again in the requisite train with Jessica joining the final one wearing the blue gown. She blew a kiss to a man that Dulcie recognized as her husband Devin in the audience. When the show concluded, the window disappeared and the looks instantly appeared on Jessica's website.

"Wow," Rachel said. She began scrolling through the images on the screen. "That was quite a transition!"

Dulcie hadn't spoken. Something was clicking in her brain but she couldn't quite make sense of it. The blue colors. The ruffles.

Rachel was still talking. "I know that color blue. I remember Bella told me it's her favorite. It's called cerulean. She said that it comes from the Latin word for 'sky'. Hey!" she said, turning to the others. "Maybe that's why Jessica called the collection *Cellestial*."

Her words rang through Dulcie's head. She quickly reached for her laptop. She opened two or three files until she found what she was looking for. There. Yes. That was it.

Dulcie politely chatted with Rachel and Francine for a moment but then said she needed to get back to work. Francine returned to the basement, and Rachel unfastened the video screen and carried it out of the room under her arm.

Dulcie shut the door and immediately called Nick.

"Where are you?" she asked. "How fast can you get over here?"

"Five minutes or so," he answered.

"Good," Dulcie said. "Is Johnson with you?"

"Yes. Should he come too?" Nick asked.

"I think so," Dulcie replied. "I've found something but I don't know how it fits quite yet. Maybe we can all put it together."

When Nick and Johnson came in they immediately sat in the chairs the women had vacated minutes before. Dulcie brought up the image on her laptop screen of Jessica James' finale dress. "Remember the designer I told you about who was a friend of Bella's in school? This is from her collection that debuted just a few minutes ago in New York."

Both men leaned forward. Neither was a fashion afficionado, and they looked confused. "Is there something specific we should notice?" Johnson finally asked.

"Not yet," Dulcie said. "Just look at the dress closely." After a moment she flipped the laptop around again and brought up another image. "What do you see here?" she asked spinning the screen back toward them.

The men leaned forward again. "That's a sketch she did of the dress," Nick finally said hesitantly, as though it was a trick question.

Dulcie nodded. "You're right. But the sketch wasn't done by Jessica. It was done by Bella a few years ago, while she was still in design school. I've been emailing with a retired professor that remembered her and sent me some of her work."

Nick and Johnson exchanged glances, then looked back at the screen. "Motive," Nick said definitively.

"That's the big piece we've been missing," Johnson added.

"But how?" asked Nick. "They weren't even around on the night of the party, right?"

Dulcie nodded. "Correct."

"Does Jessica know Antonio, or someone else who was at the party?" Johnson asked.

"I don't know," said Dulcie. "The only person I know for sure that connects them to the museum is a board member who is a colleague of Jessica's husband, Devin. And he couldn't make it to the party that night so I doubt he had anything to do with it."

They all stared at each other trying to make the mental leap from a New York designer to a London seamstress who died in Portland, Maine. It seemed impossible.

After over a minute of silence, Nick said, "Back to the drawing board. I believe we now have a case of murder. Johnson, let's get over to the station and go through everything again with the proverbial fine-tooth comb."

"Agreed," Johnson muttered, still lost in thought.

Nick turned to Dulcie. "Watch your back," he said quietly. He glanced out the window. Dan's boat was tied up to the dock. "If Dan's still around when you're done here for the day, can you just go down to the boat? I can meet you there."

Dulcie nodded. She knew why he'd asked her to do that. He didn't want her to be alone. She could feel fear beginning to creep up her spine. She watched them both leave, then quickly sent her brother a text.

'*You around this afternoon or going on a cruise later?*' she asked.

He wrote back almost instantly, '*Nope. Here for the rest of the day. Want to come down?*'

Dulcie let out a long exhale. '*Yes. Be there in about an hour,*' she wrote back.

Dan sent the smiling face with sunglasses emoji. At least he seemed to be getting back to his normal self, she thought. She was glad of that.

Less than an hour later, Dulcie was sitting on the deck of the yacht with a gin and tonic in her hand. After she'd arrived and climbed on board, her brother had offered her a beer, but the look Dulcie gave him told Dan she needed something a lot more potent.

She sipped it now gratefully as he sat down beside her. "What's going on," he said. "You look weird. Scared, even."

Dulcie realized that the ice in her glass was clinking because her hand was shaking. She took another sip and rested the glass on the rail.

"Dan, I don't want to dredge up bad memories, especially since they're so recent, but it's about Bella."

Dan shook his head from side to side to clear his thoughts and took a deep breath. "All right, what's happening now? I thought Nick and Johnson figured that out," he said.

"So did they. But it seems that now, possibly, there is motive for someone to have killed her," Dulcie told him.

"Yeah, that creep that assaulted her," Dan said.

"Nope, not him. We think it was the designer from New York that I told you about. The friend of Bella's from a while back. It looks like she copied one of Bella's designs." Dulcie explained.

"And that's motive to kill someone?" Dan exclaimed. "Seems kind of far-fetched."

"It could be motive if an entire career depends on it, and a lot of money along with that. The designer was launching a debut collection. The fashion industry can be cutthroat," Dulcie said. "Maybe almost literally in this case. The problem is, the designer wasn't anywhere near Maine when Bella died. Allergic reactions happen within minutes to hours, not days."

"So how could she do it?" Dan asked.

"We don't know," Dulcie replied. She picked up her drink and took another sip. "I hate to be a pain, but do you have any lime?" she asked.

"My sister, the refined one," Dan quipped. He went down into the cabin and emerged with a green plastic container shaped like a lime that held lime juice. He squirted it into Dulcie's drink, then began tossing it up and down like a baseball.

Dulcie swirled her drink around, watching the juice softly cloud the clear liquid.

"You should eat something with that," Dan nodded at the glass. "You probably haven't eaten all day, have you."

Dulcie realized that she hadn't. Her brother stopped tossing the lime and flipped open one of the large storage bins on the deck, pulling out a bag of potato chips. He tried to pull it open but it was glued too tightly. Dan put the top edge between his teeth and tore it open, then handed the bag to Dulcie.

She reached into it, pulled out several chips, then stopped with them midway to her mouth. She was staring at the plastic lime, now on the seat cushion beside her. Dulcie held the chips in front of her for so long that a seagull landed on the boat's stern and stared at them hungrily.

Dan laughed. "You better eat those quick!"

Dulcie stuffed them into her mouth, crunching loudly. She took a gulp of her drink. The way Dan had opened the bag with his teeth. The quick squirt of juice into her drink. Something was churning in her mind. It was right at the edge of her brain.

She saw Nick walking up the dock toward them. Dulcie took one last gulp from her glass, then handed the rest of her gin and tonic to her brother saying, "Thanks, Dan. I have to go! Talk later!"

She nearly ran up the gangplank, then broke into a sprint on the dock, thankful that she'd put on low-heeled shoes that morning. When she reached Nick she said, "I've got it! Or at least I think I've got it. But we need to find something first! We have to get back to the museum before Francine cleans everything up and throws it away!"

Nick gave her a confused look but knew it wasn't time to ask questions. He jogged along after her, wondering what could be critical enough to pull her away from what appeared to be a gin and tonic so suddenly.

Blue is the closest color to truth.

~ Steven Tyler

CHAPTER THIRTEEN

The private jet flew into Portland once again and landed on the wet tarmac. Jessica wasn't entirely happy about flying to Portland this time since it was a chilly, rainy day and the small plane had bounced around in the turbulence. Besides, she was still basking in all the accolades of her stellar New York debut and didn't want to miss a single invitation for dinner or drinks.

Devin had insisted, though. His business associate in Maine had seen her collection and was considering investing. Jessica wasn't thrilled about the financial side of fashion, but she realized that if she didn't have the money to fulfill the waves of orders now coming in, she'd never get her line off the ground. Designing and showing a collection was one thing. Getting it sold was another thing entirely.

They took a cab to the hotel, the same one that they'd stayed at before. It was nice enough, certainly, and Devin had made sure that their room had a good view of the bay.

Jessica pulled a blouse out of her overnight bag and hung it in the closet. "What time are we supposed to meet Steve?" she asked her husband.

"At two, but he told us to go over to the museum rather than his office. I guess he'll catch up with us there, then we'll head back up the street?" Devin replied.

Jessica looked out the window. The rain was coming down harder now. "Really?" she said. "He wants us to wander around the streets in this weather?" She gestured outside.

"You won't melt, Jess," Devin admonished. "And it isn't that bad. Besides, you need investors."

Jessica was annoyed. Devin was supposed to be her investor. He was, but her show had gone way over budget, so he was now scrambling for outside help. "Look, you brought your trench coat," he said. "Just throw that on with some boots and you'll be fine."

Jessica groaned and went into the bathroom to fix her hair.

CB

Antonio popped open his umbrella before emerging onto the sidewalk from his apartment building. He cleared his throat, imagining that he could feel a cold coming on. He hated this wet weather. It wreaked havoc with his voice, and he had an audition coming up in a few days.

The only reason why Antonio had agreed to meet with that museum director was because she had said the woman from the Royal Opera would be there too. Not that it had made much of a difference before. She had barely spoken with him other than to tell him he had a 'lovely voice' as she put it. No, it wasn't just lovely, it was amazing. The fact that she hadn't lavished him with gushing praise was annoying.

Then he remembered the interlude with the seamstress. He probably shouldn't have done that. Any of it, really. But he was angry at them all and felt that someone had to pay for making him feel inadequate. He was a star. They all knew it, they just wouldn't admit it.

ㄱ

Francine was already in the museum, sipping her tea. She had efficiently cleaned out the workrooms. Nothing was left except for the empty garment racks and the mostly empty trunks, waiting for the costumes to be packed back into them in a few weeks on their journey to the next leg of the tour.

Boston, then New York, then on down the coast to Washington. It would be good to get to the bigger cities, Francine thought. She liked cities. One could become lost in a city. One could remake oneself easily in a city. One could forget the past with all the distractions of a city.

Yes, she was more than ready to move on. She already had bought a ticket to take the train down to Boston the next day so that she could decide where she wanted to stay when the exhibit relocated. A new city. A new beginning.

CB

Dulcie greeted Jessica and Devin at the door of the museum. She asked them to follow her up to the boardroom. Jessica was confused. "Where's Steve?" she asked. "He was supposed to meet us here."

"Oh, he said he was running a little late," Dulcie said breezily. "He'll be along shortly."

When they entered the room, Francine was sitting at the long, heavily polished mahogany table drinking her tea. "Good afternoon!" she said as though she was expecting to see them.

"Have a seat," Dulcie said. "I'll take your coats. There's tea and coffee over there," she gestured toward a small table in the corner.

Now Jessica and Devin were both confused but obligingly sat. They glanced at each other, but Francine had already begun to make polite conversation. "I can recommend the Earl Grey," she said. "It's quite lovely." She continued, asking them about their trip from New

York, their work there, whether they had seen the exhibit downstairs….

It dawned on Devin that this woman with the refined accent who was apparently a major player with the Royal Opera might also be interested in Jessica's collection, and soon they were all engrossed in conversation.

Antonio arrived at the front of the museum and stepped under the overhanging roof of the portico. He held his umbrella sideways, opening and closing it rapidly to remove the water on it, unaware or uncaring that he was about to splash a woman passing by. She hustled along, altering her path in a wide arc to avoid his antics.

Once inside, Antonio was greeted coolly by Rachel who instructed him to follow her. He wondered why the museum director, Dr. Chambers, hadn't met him at the door. He trudged along in his overcoat, dripping on the floor.

Rachel took the coat as he entered the boardroom, shaking it firmly once to ensure that his pants got a bit wet. "Oops, sorry!" she said, smiling sweetly as she left to hang it up.

He sneered at her back, then realized that Francine was sitting at the far end of the table. His sneer became a haughty smirk and he made a bee line for the seat beside her.

Rachel returned, followed by Dulcie. Immediately behind them were Nick and Johnson. They all sat down.

"What's happening?" Jessica whispered to her husband bluntly. "Are these investors too?" she gestured toward the two men. Devin looked equally confused.

"No, we're not," Nick replied, having easily overheard. It was time to begin. "I'm Detective Nicholas Black, and this is Detective Adam Johnson. We're with the Portland Police Department."

Johnson watched everyone closely as his partner spoke. He had positioned himself near the door in case anyone attempted to jump up and run. For such a robust man, most wouldn't guess that Johnson was surprisingly quick.

Nick continued. "As many of you know, a young woman died last week. Her name was Bella Washington. She was a seamstress with the Royal Opera Company and Francine Belmont's assistant." Nick gestured toward Francine who nodded in response.

"At first Bella's death appeared to be a very unfortunate accident. She had a severe allergy to nuts, to the point where she carried two Epi-Pens with her at all times. She was always very careful about what she ate, and also made sure she had her own nutrition bars or other food with her that was not contaminated, just in case. She'd lived with the threat of this allergy for her whole life."

"What's this got to do with us?" Antonio blurted out impatiently.

"I'll explain," Nick said.

At that moment there was a knock on the door. Dulcie opened it and her brother came in, sitting down in the seat beside hers. Dan eyed Antonio with contempt.

Nick waited for Dan to sit before he continued. "On the night of the opening event, Bella was in attendance along with all of the rest of us here at this table. She had an unsettling incident take place, however, just after the performance. She had gone downstairs to the basement workroom for a moment, not realizing that Antonio had followed her down there. I'm not exactly sure what your intention was," Nick said, now looking straight at Antonio, "But you were seen kissing Bella."

"What?!?" Antonio exploded. "I never…!"

"Yes, you did," Dan now interjected. "I saw you!"

Antonio looked angrily at Dan, then around the table but said nothing.

"Bella had already rebuffed your advances, so you knew she wasn't interested, but you went ahead and forced yourself on her anyway," Nick said.

Antonio sneered for a second time in a matter of minutes. It appeared to be an expression he was familiar with making.

Nick turned to him again. "Earlier, immediately following your performance, you were seen drinking champagne and eating a piece of bread from the hors d'oeuvres table. Am I correct?" Nick said.

"I never eat or drink before a performance. It can affect my voice. I'm typically thirsty and famished immediately after," he stated bluntly.

"I see," Nick said. "So you may have been aware that the bread contained sesame seeds which are potentially deadly to someone with a nut allergy." He stopped, letting the information sink in.

The gravity of the situation began to dawn on Antonio. "Wait a minute!" he nearly shouted. "If you think I killed her... that's ridiculous! There's no way that a sesame seed in a piece of bread that I ate could kill someone that I kissed!"

"So you admit that you kissed her," Johnson said quietly.

"And yes, you can pass the allergens from food to another person by kissing them," Nick confirmed. "So you could easily have killed her."

"I'm not going to listen to this!" Antonio was actually shouting now. "It's ridiculous! I will not speak to anyone without a lawyer!"

"Fine," Nick said. "Because, you don't need to speak. You didn't actually kill Bella."

"Wait," said Devin. "Didn't you just accuse him of that?"

"No, I implied that he could have killed Bella," Nick clarified. "But he didn't. He did commit a crime by assaulting her, and she might have died from the sesame seeds, but that crime wasn't murder."

"Then why are we all here?" Jessica asked, also growing more annoyed.

"I'll explain," Nick said calmly. "Bella was always very careful to keep two EpiPens with her at all times. She knew how dangerous her allergy was. On that night, realizing that she had somehow encountered an allergen because the oncoming signs of her anaphylaxis were unmistakable, she used both pens, just as she should have."

"But she still died," Francine said quietly.

"She still died," Nick repeated. "Why?" He paused, looking around the table. Everyone was silent.

"Because the pens were old, long past their expiration date," Nick said, answering his own question.

"But why would she have old EpiPens?" Francine asked. "That puzzles me."

"It puzzled us, too," Nick said. "So we checked with her prescribing doctor who gave us the information on her pharmacy. It seems that she had picked up new ones only days before she travelled to Maine. She should have had those with her, but she didn't. Instead she had old, expired ones in her purse."

"Hadn't she replaced them with the new ones? Did she forget?" Dan now asked.

"I can answer that, I think," Dulcie said. She turned to Jessica. "Remember when I spoke with you on the phone and told you that Bella had passed away?"

"Yes," Jessica replied tentatively.

"I said that she'd had an allergic reaction," Dulcie said. "However, I never said that it was a food allergy. You told me that your husband, and I quote, 'has a food allergy, too.' Shellfish, you said. How did you know that Bella's was a food allergy?"

Jessica's face had turned pale. "I…I just assumed," she stammered. "They're so common, and Devin has one, so I didn't even think. I just…" She stopped now, her face growing very red. "Wait, you don't think…!"

"You must have known she had a food allergy because of the medical alert bracelet that she always wore, even when you were in school together," Dulcie continued, talking over Jessica's protestations. "And you probably knew that she carried the EpiPens with her. It isn't a huge stretch to imagine that your husband has them too for his allergies. You could have swapped some old ones of your husbands with the new ones in Bella's purse," Dulcie said.

"That's crazy!" Devin said, putting his arm around his distraught wife. "First of all, why would she do something like that? What motivation could she have? She hadn't seen Bella in years! And secondly, how could she possibly know that Bella would have an allergic reaction to something in the first place?"

"That's what made your plan so clever," Nick said. "You see, we finally realized that neither of you counted on Bella just randomly encountering something she was allergic to. You made sure she'd ingest something sooner or later. Preferably sooner."

"Like what?" Devin said haughtily.

"Like this," Francine said. She pulled a plastic bag out of her pocket. It contained Bella's cerulean velvet pincushion that she wore on her wrist while she worked.

"You've got to be kidding," Devin said. "She ate a pincushion?!"

Dulcie shook her head. "Of course not. But like many people who sew, she held the pins between her lips from time to time while she was working. Jessica, you knew that because you'd seen her do it in your classes with her. You've probably done the same thing yourself while you work."

"Now you're saying it was poisoned pins?" Devin said incredulously.

Dulcie ignored his outburst. "When you came to the museum and just happened to run into Bella, that wasn't a coincidence, was it. Devin, you'd carefully planned it. We've spoken with our board member Steve who said that you contacted him and suggested the meeting, not the other way around."

"Once that was set up," Dulcie continued, "You asked Steve to call me and request a preview of our new exhibit for both of you. It isn't something we typically do, but for a board member, I made an exception."

Devin was about to protest again, but Nick stopped him. "We have a signed statement from the board member in question attesting to these facts," he said very formally. Devin sat back in his chair and folded his arms.

"When you were here at the museum, while Bella was distracted showing Jessica some of the costumes, you must have had in your pocket a small eyedropper bottle or something similar with peanut oil in it. Bella had taken off the pincushion from her wrist as she did often when she wasn't actively sewing. You squeezed the peanut oil from the bottle onto the pincushion. You were lucky that it was made of a dark blue material so the oil couldn't be seen very well. It would have remained in the fabric for quite a while, coating the pins and eventually making its way into her system once she put any of the pins in her mouth."

"Seriously?!" Jessica nearly screeched. "There is no way that she could have been killed by something like that!"

"You're right, if she'd had effective EpiPens," Nick added. "But the peanut oil was only the first part of the plan. To ensure that Bella wouldn't survive, while you were distracting her as you looked at the costumes, your husband replaced her new EpiPens in her purse with old ones that would be ineffective. It isn't difficult to find a woman's purse in her workspace. It's usually in a drawer or a cupboard close to where they typically sit."

Devin was silent, but Jessica continued to fight. "And why would Devin possibly do something as contrived as all of this?" she asked.

Dulcie pulled out two pictures from a file folder. "This is why," she said quietly. The first picture was the finale dress from Jessica's new collection. The second was the sketch that Bella had done a few years before. Jessica's eyes widened as she saw the second image.

"Bella was an orphan," Dulcie explained. "When she died, she had no family and few contacts. However, Francine remembered a professor she'd spoken with who had been one of Bella's references. I got in touch with that professor and he told me how impressive Bella's work had been. He even sent me some of her sketches that he still had. Jessica, you must have made a copy of this sketch at the time Bella drew it. It's obviously identical to the finale dress in your collection."

Now turning to face Jessica and Devin directly Dulcie said, "Assuming that Bella was out of the country and long gone from the New York fashion scene, you decided to copy her work. But then one of you must have heard about the new exhibit from the Royal Opera eventually coming to New York. That must have been a nightmare scenario for you. You'd believed that Bella was out of the way in the London theater world now, far from your career in New York. You thought she would never notice that you'd used her design. But suddenly, she was going to be right back on your side of the Atlantic again, and at the worst possible time.

"Your own show in New York was already scheduled. There would still be plenty of talk about all of the fashion collections by the time the costume exhibit arrived. Bella would almost certainly hear about your show, Jessica, and probably be curious enough to see your designs online. You had to stop that from happening."

The room was silent for a moment, then the reality of the situation hit Jessica like an oncoming train. She began to gasp for air. She turned to her husband. "You said you'd take care of it!" she screeched. "She was going to recognize the dress! She'd have exposed me for stealing her work! It would have ruined my career! How could you screw this up so badly?!" Jessica screamed between ragged breaths.

"I didn't screw it up!" Devin shouted. "He did!" he pointed to Antonio. "If he hadn't gone down there and forced himself on her, no one would have even thought twice about all of this! They'd think she ate a stupid peanut or something and the EpiPens weren't enough to save her!"

Johnson stood, opening the door and nodding to a pair of uniformed officers waiting in the hallway. "The irony is," Johnson said before sitting down again, "We very nearly did." The officers quickly put handcuffs on Devin and Jessica as they removed them from the room.

Antonio had begun to push himself slowly back from the table. He now wanted to unobtrusively get out as quickly as possible.

Johnson saw him sliding from his seat. "Not so fast," Johnson said, standing again and closing the door. "You're not off the hook," he added.

Antonio's eyes were huge as he looked up at the man's large frame now looming over him "But, I didn't do it," he whined.

"Correct. You didn't kill Bella, but it appears that you did assault her. We'll need a statement from you, but I'd recommend you find a lawyer first," Johnson said.

"A good one," Dan added. "You'll need it."

"You can leave now, but don't try to leave town. We'll be in touch," Nick said. "And you'll be receiving a summons."

In addition to Anthony 'Antonio' Gallagher's fear of being in trouble with the police, he was now completely humiliated in front of a one of the major members of the Royal Opera Company. His dreams of singing at Covent Garden had been shattered. Johnson opened the door and stepped aside while Antonio stumbled from the room.

Johnson closed the door once again. "My goodness," Francine finally said. "I thought opera was dramatic!"

"I guess all those plots have to come from somewhere," Rachel quipped. "I'm still trying to wrap my head around this."

Dan nodded. "Do you really think they'd have killed Bella by lacing her pincushion with peanut oil?" he asked.

"And I'm wondering why she had the EpiPens out but her purse was back in the cupboard when she died?" Francine added.

Nick looked at Dan first. "According to our forensics team, yes it is possible, especially with the old EpiPens. It was a risk, but they were probably helped by Antonio's gaffe. It was a very clever plan though because no one, not even Devin and Jessica themselves, would have known exactly when she would have the allergic reaction. Planning a murder that takes place at a random time and when you're not even there is diabolical, to say the least."

Nick then turned to Francine. "As for the purse, we think that Bella was starting to experience an allergic reaction earlier, before the party began. We know she'd done a final fitting with Antonio that afternoon only a few hours before, and she probably had pins in her mouth from that. She had developed a rash before the anaphylaxis, so she'd probably taken out the EpiPens and put them in the pocket of her dress, just to have them ready in case she needed them immediately."

"That makes sense," said Francine. "And it reminds me of something she told me once, that a benefit of being a seamstress was she always sewed pockets into her garments if they didn't have them already. 'You never know when you'll need something right away,' she had said. I didn't realize at the time what she actually meant." Francine shook her head sadly. "Such a waste," she said. "Bella was a beautiful, talented, smart young woman. I have no doubt she could have had a brilliant career."

Dulcie looked over at Dan. He was staring down at the table, saying nothing. She knew it was time to go. He didn't need to hear any more of this.

*Blue jeans are the
most beautiful things
since the gondola.*
~ Diana Vreeland

CHAPTER FOURTEEN

The yacht rose and fell on the gentle sea at the outskirts of Portland Harbor. Dan had motored out slowly, enjoying the late afternoon sun. He caught a glimpse of his first mate Freddie's cap on the deck below, bobbing along as he walked toward the steps to the bridge. Moments later the door behind Dan opened and closed again, signaling Freddie's entrance.

"Want me to take 'er now?" Freddie asked. What was left of his gray hair peeked out randomly from under the cap.

"Sure," Dan answered. "Thanks for coming today, Freddie. I know it was kinda short notice."

"Happy to help," Freddie said, then stopped. "But I'm still gettin' paid, right?"

Dan laughed. "Yes, you're still getting paid!" he said.

Freddie looked relieved as he took the wheel. "Good, 'cause the wife says she needs to go shopping. Again."

Dan chuckled. The shopping expeditions were a weekly occurrence for Freddie. "Better you than me!" Dan said as he opened the door. Freddie just shook his head, focusing on the horizon.

Dan descended the steps and joined the others on the rear deck. It seemed like it should be a solemn occasion, but everyone looked happy. Dulcie and Nick chatted with Francine while Rachel was pouring wine. Nestled safely between the cushions was a small, engraved metal box. It almost looked like a jewelry box.

Dulcie glanced over at her brother and politely excused herself from the others. "You still good with this?" she asked as she joined him.

"Yeah," Dan said. "Bella never had family, it seems. There weren't many people that cared, or even knew anything about her. It seems like the right thing to do."

"I think you're right, and I'm glad you thought of it," Dulcie replied. She looked out at an island in the distance. "Where do you want to stop?" she asked.

"I think over by Cliff Island. Bella commented on it when we were all out here before. She said she could see herself living there," Dan said.

"Then I think it's perfect," Dulcie agreed. She gave his arm a quick squeeze. "You're a good man, Dan Chambers."

"Aw shucks," he said in response, playfully mocking her.

Within half an hour they had reached their destination. Freddie shut off the motor and kept careful watch from the bridge as the boat drifted with the current. They were quite close to land, but the bottom dropped off steeply so he knew they wouldn't run aground anytime soon.

On the rear deck, everyone stood as Dan picked up the metal box. He cleared is throat. "The last time we were all out here," he began, "Bella told me that she had always wanted to live on an island. Today I want to honor that wish. By sprinkling her ashes in the waters of Casco Bay she can choose from any of the islands here. I think she would love them all," he said. "Before we let her find her way, though, does anyone else want to add their own thoughts?"

Francine spoke up. "I never had children, but in the short time she was in my life, Bella came to feel like the daughter I should have had. I miss her already." Francine quickly dabbed her eyes.

"Bella, you rock," Rachel added. "I wish I could have known you better."

Dulcie spoke up next. "Bella, you had an impact on everyone you were with. To me you always seemed 'other-worldly' so I have no doubt you'll find your success in whatever world you're in."

They were all silent for a few moments, listening to the waves and the birds calling overhead. Dan went to the stern of the boat and opened the container. He gently tossed the ashes in a wide arc into the water.

Dulcie heard her brother whisper, "Bye, Bella. You changed me forever. I'll never forget you."

Dulcie turned to look up at Nick, standing behind her. His eyes were filled with tears. He slipped a hand around Dulcie's waist and pulled her close to him. "You've changed me forever, too," he said to her.

They watched the water sparkle as Bella's ashes drifted away. Finally, Freddie started the motor again and in the bright sunshine they slowly returned to Portland Harbor.

ଔ

The last of the trunks had been packed up carefully with the colorful costumes. The building staff were noisily hauling them down to the loading dock where a beeping truck was already backing up, waiting to take them to their next location.

Francine scurried around the dock overseeing the procedure. She checked and double-checked the numbers on each trunk to make sure that nothing was lost or forgotten. She wore jeans, a striped t-shirt and bright white sneakers. It was the first time that Dulcie had ever seen her in that sort of casual attire.

"Why, Francine! You look almost, well, American is all I can think of," Dulcie smiled.

Francine chuckled. "Rubs off on one pretty fast, wouldn't you say? But it won't last for long, so never fear."

"Nope, wasn't worried at all," Dulcie laughed. "Does this mean you're heading back to London soon?" she asked.

"Yes, I am," Francine replied. "I'll see everything set up and settled in Boston, but then I'll return home for the following month. I have a number of loose ends I need to tie up there, including interviews for a new head seamstress."

Dulcie nodded. "I know Bella can't be replaced, but I hope you find one that you like as much," she said.

"So do I, Dulcie. She's a tough act to follow," Francine admitted. "But what about you? What's next?"

"For me? Next on the agenda is our biennial of regional artists. Our committee has been narrowing down the list for the last couple of months," Dulcie replied.

"That sounds quite exciting, but I meant for you personally!" Francine looked pointedly at her friend.

"Oh!" Dulcie uttered softly. "Well, I think I've moved into a new phase of my own life," she admitted.

Francine nodded knowingly. "I thought as much. He can't take his eyes off you."

"Francine!" Dulcie exclaimed. "My goodness, it seems that everyone is intent on moving my relationship along! You'll all have me married off before the summer is over!"

Her friend laughed. "You said it first, Dulcie, not me!"

Ꮗ

Nick had taken the day off, an unusual request for him. He only told Johnson at the last minute. They were between cases now, so Johnson had plenty of extra time for additional ribbing of his partner. It was the perfect time for Nick to make his escape and complete an errand that he'd been wanting to take care of for quite some time.

He'd taken the train to Boston, getting off at North Station, then walking down the busy, winding streets until he reached the Common. He cut across it on the pathways that wound between expanses of green grass. On the other side he continued down Commonwealth Ave. The stately townhouses had long ago been divided into apartments and condominiums but still retained their external elegance. His parents owned one of them, but that wasn't Nick's destination.

Seeing the spires of Trinity Church a couple of blocks beyond, Nick cut over to nearby Newbury Street, a heavily traversed shopping district. He glanced into store windows as he walked but wasn't tempted by anything he saw. He had a single destination in mind.

At last, he reached it. A small storefront sitting back from the street, fronted by a garden with a gated entrance. Nick rang the bell. A man inside peered out the window, then buzzed Nick through.

The gate squeaked loudly as he opened it, then clanked it shut. Nick continued down a narrow path lined with roses, then entered the shop.

Glass cases glittered around him. Glistening, sparkling stones of every color were almost blinding. Nick blinked several times.

The man who had buzzed open the gate greeted him. "Mr. Black, so happy to see you!" he said.

Nick smiled. "Same to you, Mr. Goldsmith!" The fact that Mr. Goldsmith actually was a goldsmith, or more accurately, a jeweler, was not lost on anyone, including him. Goldsmiths had been among the top jewelers in Boston for generations. Nick's blueblood family had been their clients for generations as well.

"How is Mrs. Goldsmith?" Nick asked.

"She is well! Thank you for asking!" the small man exclaimed with a voice louder than one would expect from the size of his body. "We're very proud and happy to welcome a new little one into the family – our third grandchild!"

"That's great news," Nick said. "Congratulations!"

Mr. Goldsmith grinned broadly. "And how about you? Do you bring any news?" he asked, wiggling his eyebrows slightly.

Nick laughed and said, "Not as of yet, but I might soon."

"Really!" the older man said as his eyebrows raised high onto his balding head. A discreet but voracious gossip, Mr. Goldsmith knew that Nick had been ostracized from Boston society after leaving the family law firm to work as a detective and, perhaps even more scandalous, having the audacity to divorce his well-connected wife.

Nick understood very well that Mr. Goldsmith knew every detail of his recent past. Well, nearly every detail. Nick was about to give him a new and quite juicy bit of news to savor and circulate in the coming days.

"Yes," Nick continued. "No news quite yet, but I was wondering if you could show me the diamonds. The rings, to be precise."

Mr. Goldsmith jingled the keys on a large ring that he kept attached to his beltloop. "I would be very happy to, Mr. Black!" he nearly shouted. "Step right over this way!"

Nick grinned as he followed the man between the cases. Yes, at last, it was finally happening.

The Dulcie Chambers Mysteries

Book #1
An Exhibit of Madness
(Previously titled: *Portrait of a Murder*)

Dr. Dulcinea (Dulcie) Chambers has a lot on her mind. She's just opened a new exhibit of Winslow Homer watercolors at the Maine Museum of Art where she's Chief Curator. The exhibit will be complete when the museum's director, the urbane Joshua Harriman, buys the final piece at auction. But when Dulcie discovers a body where the painting should have been, she's one of the primary suspects. Portland Police Detective Nicholas Black is on the case but finds he is less than objective when it comes to the attractive Dr. Chambers.

Book #2
From the Murky Deep

Detective Nicholas Black has cause for concern. He's investigating the suspicious death of a young woman whose body has just washed on shore in full scuba gear. Normally it would simply be a case of drowning, yet along with this particular body is a stolen Vincent van Gogh painting in a watertight tube. To further complicate matters, the phone number of Dr. Dulcinea (Dulcie) Chambers is written on the dead woman's hand. As the new director of the Maine Museum of Art, Dulcie is already busy negotiating the sale of one of the museum's pieces with a wealthy collector. When Dulcie learns that she's a chief suspect however, she has no choice but to help with the investigation. Dulcie finds herself diving in to solve this mystery as her relationship with Detective Nicholas Black also reaches new depths.

Book #3
The Fragile Flower

World-renowned abstract expressionist painter Logan Dumbarton is welcomed to the Maine Museum of Art to teach a master class to a group of talented local artists. But he proves more difficult than any of the staff, along with his stunning yet whiny wife and his spinster/business-manager sister, can handle with his constant complaints and egocentric demeanor. Within a week the entire class loathes him. Is he really worth all this trouble? Somebody doesn't seem to think so and it's up to Dr. Dulcinea ("Dulcie") Chambers to find out who. But she'll have to team up with Detective Nicholas Black once again, and their relationship at the moment can only be described as *fragile*.

Book #4
A Mind Within

While assembling a new exhibit featuring *Art Brut* or "Outsider Art," Dr. Dulcinea ("Dulcie") Chambers encounters an enormously talented and equally troubled young man, Xander Bellamy. An autistic savant, Xander has not communicated with anyone for several months, since his father was sent to prison for the murder of Xander's domineering grandfather. Detective Nicholas

Black thought the case was closed until Dulcie came to him with compelling evidence that the real killer was still at large. When evidence had originally pointed to Xander as the murderer, Xander's father had quickly confessed. Did he do this to save his son from being committed to a mental institution for the criminally insane? Xander's battle-axe aunt has come to live with him and, along with long-time family housekeeper Giselle, they see to his needs. But is there more to them than meets the eye? Meanwhile Dulcie seeks to see inside Xander's mind with the help of psychologist Dr. Raymond Armand. However, the ambitious Armand has other ideas about the lovely Dr. Chambers and is about to give Nicholas Black some competition when it comes to her affections.

Book #5
Last of the Vintage

Dr. Dulcinea Chambers' old boyfriend, the adventurous, fun-loving, and decidedly good-looking Brendan MacArthur, reappears with a unique gift for the Maine Museum of Art: a very old bottle of wine, one of several that he found in a shipwreck while scuba diving in Maine's cold Atlantic waters. With museum attendance low during a particularly brutal winter, Dulcie knows exactly what to do. The museum will host a wine tasting as a fundraiser featuring this old vintage. But when an icebreaker busts through the pack ice in Portland harbor the day after the festivities, the crew makes a gruesome discovery. Someone from the party didn't make it home, and instead wound up among the bobbing gray-blue sheets of ice floating from one side of the harbor to the other.

Dulcie's knowledge of wine is needed by detective Nicholas Black as he sorts through the details of this case, but their budding relationship is also put to the test. Brendan MacArthur's sudden reappearance irritates Nick. Does he ignore his feelings and chalk them up to simple jealousy, or is there something else far more dangerous about this Brendan MacArthur that Dulcie and Nick have yet to discover?

Book #6
The Hand That Feeds You

As if running an art museum wasn't enough, Dr. Dulcinea Chambers now finds herself in battle with the new board of directors chair, Vanessa Rich, who is on a ruthless quest to trim the budget in any way she can. Her cost-cutting measures will begin with selling off Dulcie's antique office furniture, much to Dulcie's bewilderment. Detective Nicholas Black is no less perplexed when falconry expert Esmerelda Graves barges into the police station insisting that one of her prized birds has been murdered.

Ulterior motives are certainly at play as Dulcie finds that Vanessa stands to profit from the sales, while Nick learns that Esmerelda's raptors are carrying tiny video cameras. When the seemingly disconnected worlds of these two shady women begin to intertwine, and a most certainly murdered person turns up where the dead bird was found, Dulcie and Nick need hawk-like precision to determine why… before someone else falls prey.

If you would like to read the Dulcie Chambers Mysteries please visit the author's website (kerryjcharles.com) for more information or request copies at your local bookstore or library. Ebook versions are also available from major suppliers online.

Reviews from thoughtful readers are always welcome on any website or media outlet. Thank you!

ABOUT THE AUTHOR

Kerry J Charles has worked as a researcher, writer, and editor for *National Geographic*, the Smithsonian Institution, Harvard University and several major textbook publishers. She holds four degrees including a Masters in Geospatial Engineering and a Masters in Art History from Harvard University. She has carried out research in many of the world's art museums as a freelance writer and scholar.

A swimmer, scuba diver, golfer, and boating enthusiast, Charles enjoys seeing the world from above and below sea level as well as from the tee box. Her life experiences inspire her writing and she is always seeking out new travels and adventures. She returned to her roots in coastal Maine while writing the Dulcie Chambers Mysteries.